A Well Travelled Notebook

A Well Travelled Notebook
A Second Collection of Tales and Poems from West Lothian Writers

Editors:

Anne E. Edwards
Norman Geddes
Eric McFarlane
Stephen Shirres
Sally Thomson

West Lothian Writers
2015

First Printing: 2015

ISBN 978-1-326-47666-3

www.westlothianwriters.org.uk

Contents

Foreword

West Lothian Writers was founded in 2006 and since then we have grown in numbers and experience. Every fortnight new and varied writing is presented by members to the group for enjoyment and critique. This book contains many examples of such writing.

The original plan was to select one piece of work from each contributor, however the quality of the work made this difficult so there are several examples from each of our authors.

At the back of this book you'll find more information about West Lothian Writers and how we support our members.

We hope you enjoy reading the pieces here as much as we did when selecting them.

Time Zones
Ian Macartney

Eating dinner at midnight,
waking up fast asleep.

The darker the night,
the lighter the blue.
On another decimal
a similar ink poem
hugs the stars.

There are times when the ocean separates
into strands of chatspeak ,
times when the clock doesn't tick.

There we transcend time,
make order into stuff and
talk about the stuff and
sometimes the stuff isn't the planned stuff
but it's still discussed stuff
so it becomes timeless beautiful

memory.

The conversation is where oceans stop.

Number, colon, number,
replaced with beautiful letters.

A walk like no other
Sue Davies

Fifteen minutes from my friends house to the last parked car, the only parked car. Then five along the pine needled and puddled road looking for the left turn. Not the aluminium gate maybe, no - minute or two further left through the kissing gate, wood still pale and unmingled with evidence of long use. A grassy track beyond has been somewhat used as the snow is worn and shiny, slick, to be avoided unless too wide to skirt and requiring a cracking crossing with firm boots.

The light is just right for my photo chromic specs to show no difference, bar blurring the effect without them, in the deeply warm cerise tones of the birch twigs haloing round the irregular verticals of white bark and the nearer glowing of a sphagnum burial ground with the customary dome. Turning round and looking up above the white Meall-a-Bhuillin the pale blue skies were cut through with shining transient lines and subtler-than-candy-floss-pink clouds caught by the four o'clock sun in late January.

Gently rounding the hill each rise in elevation brings changes underfoot; more snow, crunchier to the depth of a boot, then harder, the tread barely breaking the crust but giving sure footing. Steps up and over the fence reach the heather held muddy lines marked here and there by a narrow tyre.

Aiming for a round route I nearly give up finding the stony path I know well but give it four more minutes and find it in three. Here the less dense pines are gracefully spaced, the exposed stones

2

start sounding my boots and one sweet tweet foregrounds the whispering wind wheeling and searching and cooling the lobes of my ears.

I turn right on the path I know has a steeper descent and only grey and blue tones now accompany the six-eight chime of my boots, which is the rhythm to the choir's tune I am becoming familiar with, mixed with old, old hymns that return from childhood stalls.

The car is gone. Returning to Tarmac, coloured lights and the echo of axe on wood bring human kind back into focus. One blackbird alarms and the wind and the shushing river merge with the silence in aleatoric time.

Just a walk, but a walk like no other because it was this walk, this late January day, this place, this year, with these songs in my head, Ubi Caritas .... Dear Name the Rock....La la la........la la, La la la........la la... I sing and the latch clicks.

Homecoming
Norman Geddes

Bernard Marchant glanced at his watch but couldn't make sense of it. From the bus window he looked out on busy pavements. Winter darkness was splashed everywhere with the brilliant light from shop windows. Another two stops and then he was almost home. 'Daddy, Daddy, Daddy! You know what I did today?' He smiled in anticipation. The smell of dinner being cooked, a kiss from Dora . . .

'Mr Marchant, hello! Do you remember me?'

He turned from the window and looked at a woman in mid 30's in navy business suit and smartly styled dark brown hair. Vaguely, he recognised her. She helped him out. 'Mary Crawford? Heatherfield High School?'

'Of course! Mary! How are you getting on?' This conversation puzzled him despite his pleasure in encountering her. He'd been speaking to her after class that very morning.'

'Well I'm now Mary Irving and I've got two grown up children. I'm a woman in a man's world, Mr Marchant, I'm an architect.' The bus heaved into a bus stop. 'Oh I have to go, this is my stop. Collecting my car from the garage. Cheerio, Mr Marchant, nice to have met you ...' And she was gone, her heels cling on the stairs.

'After the Republic who was Rome's first emperor? Shand?'

'Julius Caesar, sir.'

'Nope. He certainly paved the way but ... yes, Mary?'

'Augustus, sir.'

'*Augustus,* yes indeed!' Bright girl, Mary Crawford.

A very bright girl. He rose from his seat because the next stop was his. He stepped off the bus and felt a twinge of pain in his chest. Nothing unusual there, he had twinges of pain everywhere these days; knees, hips, shoulders. He walked along the busy pavement confident he was almost home yet uncomfortably aware that the street was somehow unfamiliar. He waited at the traffic lights for an opportunity to cross the road and glanced up at the building opposite. His living room window was on the corner of the tenement and looked down on this cross-roads. The lights changed and people began hurrying across the road in both directions. Bernard stood transfixed, staring up at a towering building of greenish glass ablaze with fluorescent lighting. People jostled him in their rush, he was unaware of them.

Then a man's voice at his shoulder said, 'Can I be of any help sir? You're looking a bit lost'

Bernard turned and looked at the policeman.

'You're looking a bit lost, Marchant, would you like someone to take your hand?'

'I'm not lost, Sarge.'

'Well your fucking feet are! Left right, left right!'

'Er no. Thank you, I'm fine.' The truth was beginning to dawn on Bernard. 'It's a long time since I've been in this part of town. That glass building ... where the hell did that come from?'

The policeman smiled. 'It's been there a fair few years.'

'Has it really?' Bernard was amazed. 'I used to live there. Ah well, there you are. Times change, eh?'

'They do indeed, sir. Now, are you sure you're OK?'

'Thank you, yes. I go this way ...'

Another bus. No more confusion, this time he knew exactly where he was going. He smiled to himself. Going to be late though and Dora will wonder what on earth has happened. Again he smiled to himself while he pictured the scene ahead of him. Dora would have switched on all the lamps in the lounge and the curtains would be drawn across the bay window. Cosy. He would dump his brief case in the study, get rid of his jacket and tie and join her in a small sherry while they watched the news. Then dinner. Brief case! Where is it? Oh, God, I must have left it in the classroom and I've got Third Years homework to mark. Tough! I'll do it tomorrow.

In the seat directly in front of his own two women held a loud conversation about their recent holidays. 'It was wonderful,' said one, 'Rome in August ...'

'What sort of an emperor was Augustus? Good or bad? Opinions, please?'

'He was ...'

He stopped Mary politely. 'I think it is time we had a contribution to these proceedings from Ross Fulton. Ross?'

'What?'

'I want you tell us whether you think Augustus was a good or bad emperor.'

Fulton shrugged. 'Sorry, I wouldn't know. Unlike you I wasn't around at the time.'

'Stand up, Fulton.'

'Eh?'

'On your feet now!'

The boy shambled insolently to his feet.

Bernard grabbed a magazine from the desk. 'Not really much interested in history, are you, Fulton.' Already he was aware that this detestable boy was about to crack his temper.

'Nah, pretty boring really.'

'Your mind is taken up by altogether loftier matters, I suppose? Like this!' He held the magazine up displaying its nude woman to the class. There were giggles and some raucous laughter. The boy grinned defiantly but a red tinge spread upwards through his face and this, perhaps, spurned Bernard on.

6

After the event Bernard was unable to remember much of what he said. He heard his own voice rise and his face was so close to Fulton's that all he could make out were the boy's diverted eyes and the bridge of his nose. Ross Fulton was in fact very close to tears which he may have tried to avert with a deliberate loss of temper.

'Back off, you old poof! You're too close for comfort!'

Bernard grabbed him by his jacket collar and hauled him out from behind his desk. 'We'll settle this in the corridor, right now!'

'I'd like to go back to Italy,' the woman on the bus told her friend, 'but David's keen to do France. I think it's so important to avoid the Spanish Costas, don't you?'

'Things don't look good, Bernard.'

'Alastair, I did not strike the boy. He made to strike *me*. I merely placed my hands on his shoulders to restrain him when he gave this almighty yell and threw himself on the floor.'

The headmaster cleared his throat. 'He has a gash on his face.'

'He got that from a radiator when he threw himself down.'

'What on earth were you thinking about? You should have kept you temper in check and sorted the matter out inside the classroom.'

Bernard nodded his head submissively. 'Retrospective wisdom, Alastair; too late to be of any use.'

'I fear so, Bernard, I fear so.'

Off the bus he walked along a broad tree lined street, leafy in summer but now, in mid November, just dark and soggy. It was good to be home at last.

He opened the garden gate and walked up the path to the front door, reaching into his pocket for the key. Couldn't find it. Tried all his pockets. Strange. He pressed the doorbell and waited for Dora to answer it. He would have a laugh, pretend to be a rag and

bone man. As soon as the door began opening he called out in a
loud voice, 'Any auld clothes, love ...' And then his jaw dropped.

A tall man, balding and dressed in a green check shirt and
fawn cardigan frowned but then, perhaps seeing Bernard's look of
astonishment, gave a cautious smile.

'Who are you?' Bernard asked him.

'Shouldn't I be asking you that question?' said the man.

'I'm Bernard Marchant. I live here.'

'Do you really. Well in that case you'd better come in.'

Deeply confused Bernard followed the tall man along a
hallway both familiar and unfamiliar. In the large lounge beige
curtains were closed across the bay window. Dora had hung cream
ones with roses. The three piece suite was chunky and leather.
Theirs had been maroon moquette. The furniture was sparse
compared to the clutter Bernard remembered.

To his host Bernard said, 'Look, I'm awfully sorry but ...'

'Do sit down, Mr Marchant.'

'Bernard lowered himself onto the settee. '... I've come to the
wrong door . . . silly of me ...'

The man settled himself in an armchair and smiled. 'This
room must seem very different?'

Bernard allowed his eyes to roam, nodding his head as he did
so.

'What about the fireplace?' he was asked.

Marble mantelpiece, black iron centre with mock-coal gas
installation and square tiles with Dutch scenes down either side.
Bernard leaned forward, peering carefully. 'Pity about that crack,
isn't it?'

'Crack?' said the man.

'The tiles on the right,' said Bernard, 'third tile down, there's a
very faint hairline crack cunning across the lower left corner.'

'Ah yes, that. It's unfortunate but barely noticeable. Unless, of course, you live here.'

'Y-e-s. Look, I'm very sorry to have bothered you like this ...' He made to get up but the man raised his hand to stop him.

'I'm Roger. Roger Fox. My wife and I moved into this house six years ago. I was surprised and delighted when I discovered that it had once been the home of Bernard Marchant. I'm something of a fan, you see.'

'A fan?'

'Hadrian's Frostbitten Servant, The Reluctant Freedman... Wonderful novels, Bernard.'

'You can't resign.'
'I have no choice, Dora.'

'You can fight this!'

'I can't.'

'How will we live, for God's sake?'

'My novel, The Baths Attendant ... it looks as if it'll be published.'

'Oh whoopee do! Nobel Prize for literature here we come!'

'I'll get a job. I'll work in a book shop or something like that.'

'You know what I do for a living, Bernard? I'm an academic. University Professor. Subject? Classics.'

Bernard's jaw dropped. Then he smiled. He felt as if all the exploded fragments of his mind had suddenly re-formed, like pieces of a jigsaw. 'You know, Roger, I always dreaded being confronted by genuine authorities on the subject. And here you are telling me you are a fan?'

'Absolutely.' He seemed about to expand on this but, instead, asked, 'Bernard, would you like something to drink? I've a fully stocked drinks cabinet and I can also rise to tea or coffee.'

'Well actually, Dora and I usually have a wee sherry at this time.'

'Of course,' said Roger.

But Bernard shook his head violently. 'I'm talking nonsense again. Dora's been dead for ... I can't remember ...'

'In that case,' said Roger, 'you and I shall have a wee sherry in her memory. How's that?'

Bernard smiled happily. 'You're very kind,' he said.

While Roger poured their drinks Bernard felt again that pain in his chest. It wasn't severe and is was a pressure rather than a pain. Nevertheless, he had the impression that it was an ominous warning. He hoped that it was and cheerfully ignored it.

'My wife is out this evening. Some sort of Ladies gathering. I have to see to myself. Plenty of these microwave meals in the freezer, Bernard ...' He handed his guest a sherry in a schooner. 'Somewhat ghastly, really, but when needs must and all that ... but if we feel hungry I can provide.'

Bernard raised his glass. 'Cheers. And thank you for your very considerate hospitality.' The pain came back just then but he hid it well.

'Cheers,' said Roger. And then, 'Do you have family, Bernard? Sons, daughters, that sort of thing?'

'Hm, yes. Angus, he's a chemical engineer, lives with his wife and two sons in Linlithgow. And Rachael, she's a radiographer at ... ' But Roger was no longer listening and at a suitable pause, he excused himself, went into the hall promising to be just a couple of minutes.

'Are you hungry yet, Bernard?' he asked when he returned.

'No. But a refill of that lovely sherry would go down very well.' The pain, pressure or whatever it was had come back stronger than ever.'

'Of course,' said Roger as he moved back towards the drinks cabinet. 'We were talking, as I recall, about academics and novelists ...'

'Ah yes, so we were. I did actually study history you know? Did a post grad then went into teaching.'

'Why teaching?'

'I believed I had a talent for it. But I was wrong.'

Roger smiled, shook his head and threw one leg over the other. 'So, you gave up teaching, turned to writing historical novels and continued to teach.'

'Actually I gave up teaching to work in a book shop.'

'And yet, you continued teaching through your novels.'

Bernard took a sip of sherry. 'I only set out to entertain.'

'And you do! You engage the imaginations of people who would never otherwise come within a million miles of Roman history. That is a great thing.'

They talked about Roman history for well over an hour and Bernard quite forgot how he came to be in this house. Occasionally he found himself trying to remember when he and Dora had redecorated and why they had chosen this rather awful leather suite. But he liked his guest, this Roger fellow whoever the hell he was, and became completely engrossed in their conversation. The pain in his chest was tightening its grip. He found himself having to breath more deeply, something he tried to hide from Roger. And then came the shrill ring of the doorbell.

'Ah,' said Roger, smiling, 'this I believe is someone for you.' And he rose from his chair and left the room.

The pain had served to rearrange once more Bernard's confused thoughts. This was not his house, Dora had not chosen

this awful suite. Nor had they drank cream sherry! Always dry.
He could hear muttered voices coming from the hall, a hushed
conversation.

And then Dora walked into the room and his pain seemed to
ease.

'Honestly, Bernard, you never manage to close these curtains
properly.' There was a smile in her voice as she moved to the
curtains and adjusted them where they came together. 'Now,' she
said, 'I'll get us both a sherry if you'll give the fire a poke then put
another lump of coal on.'

Bernard rose to attend to the fire.

Moments later the door was pushed open. 'A visitor for you,
Bernard. Your grandson. Bernard? Oh my God!'

Bernard was lying in front of the fire place. They never did
manage to work out why he was clasping the ornamental poker.

Abraham King's Writing Desk
Stephen Shirres

Linlithgow Gazette | Friday October 24 2014
Deaths
KINGSTON Abraham Patrick died peacefully on 15th October 2014 aged 74 after a short illness. Husband of the late Stephanie Kingston and father of Carrie and Debbie. Funeral service at St Michael's Church, Linlithgow on Wednesday 5th November at 11am. Family flowers only but, if desired, donations for Poppyscotland may be sent to W. F. Massie Funeral Directors, 15 Summerfield Terrace, Linlithgow, EH49 6SU.

Carrie's Diary
14/11/2014

Tomorrow is the day. The first day back in their house without either of them. It changed when mum died, the atmosphere I mean. The warmth, however much Dad tried, was duller. He continued Mum's tradition of having a pot of coffee on at all times but after a while he stopped when no one came round to drink it. Mum was the one who had house visitors. All Dad's friends lived in the pub or at the football. The house became untidy and dominated by cigars.

Now it looks and smell like a show house thanks to the funeral. Debs and I tidied the main rooms so we can hold the funeral tea at the house. The first time the place had been properly alive since Mum's funeral. Weird how a good funeral can be a wonderfully happy event.

Whatever the place is like, it won't change my memories. In many ways it was the perfect childhood home with a huge garden filled with hidey-holes and trees to climb. We even had our own fairy tale villain. I'm sure Farmer Donald was a perfectly nice guy. He just wouldn't leave us alone. We'd be having a tea party in the garden or a paper airplane competition and he'd keep trying to talk to us. We'd more important things to worry about.

Debs being Debs has just text me asking if I've booked the van. Of course I have, I've got all the paper work sitting beside me. God I look terrible in my driving license photo. Thank you Scottish weather for that one, didn't realize that when you renewed your driving license they took a new photo. I looked a right state after walking through the wind and rain to get to the post office. The reason we have the van is to get rid of the big stuff ASAP so we have more room to work in. Neither of us need the so far out of fashion it is almost vintage sofa while I'm pretty sure Dad's old reading chair will fall apart when we try and move it. If everything goes to plan I'll be making multiple trips to the dump and the local charity shops.

Sam offered to come with me. He even said he'd drive the van but we decided that the first trip should just be me and Debs. He was our father at the end of the day.

Carrie's Phone

DEBS: Hi Carrie. Walking up to the house now. Bus was early for once. What's your eta? Dx
SAT 10.18

DEBS: At the house now. Shame the rain was early as well. Bloody soaking. Putting a coffee on. Do you want one? Dx
SAT 10.23

DEBS: Where are you? Dx
SAT 10.25

CARRIE: 3 missed calls? Seriously Debs! I was driving & this van is almost as old as u! I'll skip the coffee as you'll burn it as usual xox
SAT 10.31

DEBS: I never burn coffee! Dx
SAT 10.32

Carrie's Diary
15/11/2014
I'm glad that is over and done with. The house felt like a shell, a museum that nobody cared about, and we only made it worse. We made the walls bare and emptied rooms while filling others to the max, like a storage locker.

For once I was glad Debs burnt her coffee. She made the place smell like Mum. I felt she was by our side as we sorted and shifted. All that was missing was Dad. Next time I might leave one of his cigars smouldering in one of his ash trays. Neither of us could throw out the two and a half packets we found in his bedroom.

One nice bonus was getting to take Dad's writing desk home with me. There was always something magical about it. It was his and no one else's. Even Mum never got to see what was locked away in those drawers. I made sure I found the key before I left. Going through it is tomorrow's job. I already feel a guilty excitement about digging through such a secret place.

Carrie's phone

CARRIE: Debs Pick up ur bloody phone! U'd think 3 missed calls would be a clue that i wanted 2 talk 2 U! It is important! It is about Dad & us! Call me back will U!!!!!!!!! xox
SUN 10.47

First Page of A Notebook Found in Abraham Kingston's Writing Desk

~~Dear my Gorgeous Twins~~ Dear Carrie and Debbie,

You are the greatest things ever to happen to your mother and I

~~Dear Carrie and Debbie,~~

~~I am writing to you~~

Dear Carrie and Debbie,

I am sorry I am unable to tell you this news in person. If I had the strength to do so I would. It is not your response I am afraid of but speaking the words out loud.

Dear Carrie and Debbie,

I am sorry I am unable to tell you this news in person. You both deserve better.

When I read his letter, ~~it did not make me love you any less~~ if it is possible, it made me love you even more

Dear Carrie and Debbie,

I love you

Letter found in Notebook from Abraham Kingston's Writing Desk

M Donald
Preston Road Farm
Linlithgow
9th January 1981

Dear Stephanie,

I am deeply sorry I have to write to you like this, especially after your last letter its good news. No one be told something so happy and then never talked to again. Did you think I would happily disappear into the night once I heard you were pregnant with our children?

I want, no I need to talk to you about all of this. If I was ever in a crisis you would be the first person I would turn to. Now I'm in one and you blank me. In the end I had to say something. I hope Abraham does not see this letter. Does he know?

Please speak to me Stephanie. I need to know where we go from here. Our relationship can not just stop now there are now physical consequences. I should not call them that but that is what they are. They are my DNA as much as yours. In fact twins run in my family. Our family now. I want to bring up my children, a dream I've always had.

Please reply Steph, I need to know.

Yours as always

M.

Carrie's Diary
16/11/2014
I still can't believe it. I've read the letter four or five times but the words never go in. The sit above my understanding like oil on water. How can Dad not be my Dad?
Hopefully once I show the letter to Debs the whole thing will feel more real. Or at least real enough to deal with it. I just wish she'd call me back.

Carrie' Diary
17/11/2014...well 18th really
Just back from Debs'. I should be in bed but my mind is still buzzing. Debs took it badly tears followed by anger at me! I didn't make Mum sleep with that........oh I don't know what to bloody call

him. His time should be about Dad, not ripping him out our lives for a second time in a month!

Debs wanted to rush round and confront Farmer Donald and have it out with him at 11 at night. She only didn't go because I pointed out he hadn't lived next to Mum and Dad's for almost 25 years. She didn't take the news well. She never likes me correcting her. That's when the anger and the bitches started. Why the hell is she angry at me? It was Mum's fault. I didn't choose to be that Man's daughter. Stupid woman...both of them Debbie and Mum!

Carrie's phone

DEBS: Sorry I was such a bitch last night Carrie. I know you understand but I wanted to say anyway. I didn't mean half the stuff I said. Dx
TUE 00.02

CARRIE: You weren't Debs. I was. I should never have said those things about Mum. Call u 2night? 7pm? Xox
TUE 7.34

DEBS: You better bitch ;-)
Dx TUE 8.13

Carrie's Diary
18/11/2014 (the real 18th)
Despite my nervous the phone call went well. I almost hung up while the number dial. Of course we touched on last night but not the words. If we'd been face to face we'd have probably hugged it out but her kind words are a good second.

Debs being Debs has already got a plan but she wanted me to sign off on it. Miracles do happen! She is going to find Farmer Donald's new address. While she does that I'm to write him a letter from the two of us. For all we know he hasn't thought about us since the 80s so lets give him a chance to ease himself back in. I've never written one of those letters. Where the hell do I start?

Carrie's phone.
DEBS: What are the chances that Donald's first name is Mac? Dx
THU 19.47

CARRIE: No parent would do that to a child. Social services would be on them like a flash for child abuse lol xox
THU 19.54

DEBS: I wood Dx
THU 19.55

CARRIE: & that is Y I fear for ur unborn child xox
THU 19.59

Carrie's Diary
22/11/2014
First time back at Mum and Dad's since I found the letter. On one level it didn't feel any different. The house felt more like a shell as we sorted and shifted all their stuff. As a memorial to Dad's we lit one of his unused cigars and left it smouldering in an ash tray. The smell was wonderful, nostalgia and family. We each took a cigar home with us. Mine lives in the glass of important things by my bed joining my Scottish £1 note and the first thing Sam gave me, a

Lego man that supposedly looks like me. Apart from sharing the same shade of artificial red hair I don't see the likeness.

Debs mentioned the letter. I said I'd written a draft which is a small white lie. I've got a few ideas jotted in Dad's notebook - the closest I'm going to get to his help on this one. She is further ahead. She has a whole bunch of address which she is slowly narrowing down. I'm not sure I want to know how.

Carrie's Diary

27/11/2014

Debs has found his address. Claims she's seen a phone of him as well. He isn't looking good according to her. Not surprising considering how old he looked when we were children. The problem now is Debs wants to send the letter but I've barely written a first draft.

I brought myself some time by saying I'd show her something on Saturday which she agreed to much to my shock. I guess i better stop wasting time writing this and get on with what I'm actually meant to be doing. Here goes nothing.

Carrie's Phone

CARRIE: What address should I put on the letter Debs? Your's or mine? Xox
THU 23.36

DEBS: No idea. I hadn't thought of that. Can't we include a joint email? Dx
THU 23.37

CARRIE: Email? Farmer Donald must be well into his eighties. He won't know how to use email. Probably doesn't even have a computer xox
THU 23.40

DEBS: U R being ageist. I bet he knows how to use a computer find Dx
THU 23.41
DEBS: Fine I mean. Damn autocorrect.
THU 23.41
DEBS: If we are going to put a postal address, do you want to use mine as it is closer to his home at the mo DX
THU 23.42

CARRIE: Good idea lass. U have sum use after all ;-) xox
THU 23.46

Letter Addressed to Mr R MacDonald

Carrie and Debbie Kingston
c/o 15 Smithfield Road
Glasgow
G14 7AS
29/11/2014

Dear Mr MacDonald

Our names are Carrie and Debbie Kingston. We recently discovered the letter you wrote to our mum Stephanie Kingston on the 9th of January 1981.

We agree that the matter touched on in your letter should be discussed face to face. If you would still like to meet us please suggest a time and place and we will meet you there.

One thing we would like to add however, is that whatever the truth maybe we will not let you replace the man we consider to be our father, Abraham Kingston. If you are happy to agree to this please contact us using the phone number or email address below.

Yours sincerely

Carrie and Debbie Kingston

Carrie's diary
30/11/2014
The letter has been posted and it was all an anti-climax really. Nothing happened, nothing changed. Throughout this whole thing very little seems to have changed. Dad still feels like Dad. Mum still feels like Mum. Even the anger I felt towards her has soften. As Sam would say, no point in feeling angry towards the dead. Whether Dad was a bad husband or Donald was a brilliant lover it didn't matter, what is done is done. It doesn't change that Dad did all the hard work.
The question now is the reply. Debs knows she wants one. I think I'd like one too but I don't know why. The man can't be a father to us and we aren't after that or money. The best we all get is the truth whatever that is worth.

Linlithgow Gazette | Friday December 5 2014

Deaths
MacDONALD, Robert Joseph died peacefully on Saturday 29 December aged 86. The funeral will take place at Falkirk Crematorium on Tuesday 9 December at 12.45pm. Enquiries to the Crematorium

Corra Linn
Sally Thomson

Windy down hill road
Narrows as we take the last bend
Past terraced houses
We drive further down hill
Late evening, sun is still shining
We park the car, set out on our walk

All is still now
In the cotton mill village
Once an industrial community
A model of utopia
Bustling with men, women and children

All is quiet now
The beating of cotton looms
I can hear faintly
In the distance of my mind
Mill buildings and tenements stand, stern and self-righteous
Soaring out from the gorge
Many a tale to be told
Of toil and comforts of another time

River flowing near
Water wheel turning
Dripping as it goes round and round
Beads glistening in the evening sun

We walk between buildings

The river urging us on our way
Up stone steps into woodland
Fresh smell of lavender, beech and pine
A cooler, greener, darker place

Once through the stone doorway
A weir and lookout point
Water, tinged with golden brown
Roaring down, swirling, crashing over rocks
Whistling like wind blowing trees, leaves trembling
Boisterous surging with recent rain

By the river's edge we walk
The whistling fades
Pine needles underneath our feet
The boardwalk twists round tree roots
The water calm and still

Thistle, foxglove, hogweed, meadow sweet
Bramble sprawls under pine, beach and sycamore
Trees tall and slender towering above
Leaves of fern curl at their roots

Otter, badger, bat
Kingfisher, woodpecker, peregrine falcon
Trout, stickle back, pike
Toad and butterfly
Hawthorn, oak, rowan, ash
Willow, elm and birch
Nature's generosity all around

Birdcall high over our heads

Sun shines through a canopy above
Shapes and shades of green
Weave patterns in the sky
Pink purslane, forget-me-not at our feet
A wild red currant stands alone by the river's edge
Berries jewels in the rich green surrounds

An opening and there is the cottage by the Clyde
Window baskets in full bloom
Walled garden across the path
Humming of generators to our left
Bonnington Power Hydro to our right
The big white building
We pass as we walk

Water rushes
Purple, white and yellow of thistle and daisy
Dance up hill
Caressing sides of long pipes as they slope down
Fresh smell of pine, beech and moss
We climb into woodland
A cooler, greener, darker place

Up the stony dirt path
Water beckoning as we near
Evening sun beacons over the cliffs edge, down through trees
The hidden beauty slowly appears
Gorge and its river surging down steep steps
Crashing against rocks
Rowdy, rolling with spit
Fast water flows and swirls
Onwards racing round rocks

Nature at full force
The sound and beauty of Corra Linn

Edinburgh Fringe
Jenifer Harley

Buzz Buzz, Chatter Chatter, Clink Clink, Woo!
Late summer in the capital is a hullabaloo.
Fantastic just to get there for the atmosphere is braw,
Bus station, Train station, taxi, tram, rickshaw

Laugh Laugh, Chortle Chortle, Clink Clink, Wow!
Come along to makeshift theatres like the upside down cow.
From Assemblies to Balloons, crowds surge up and down the hill
Side shows, Street shows, knife swallowers thrill.

Walk Walk, Hurry Hurry, Clink Clink, Whee!
The show is about to start and you might get in for free.
Fresh artists will perform in back rooms on every street
New plays, Old plays, keen thespians meet.

Shhh Shhh, Quiet Quiet, Clink Clink, Shhh!
Lights are going down, anticipated curtain swooshhh.
The act appears on stage to cheers from a pumped-up crowd
Bad jokes, Heard jokes, comedian's shroud

Up Up, On On, Clink Clink, awaits.
The next hostelry is not too far, we must get good seats
A line is snaking from the door; the place is fit to burst,
Push Push, Jostle, Jostle, we were here first.

Booked Booked, Sold Out Sold Out, Clink Clink, Boo!
Go on over the High Street to a Pleasance venue.
Above, Below, Beyond, Beside, round the corner to the Grand
Queue, Queue, Wait, Wait; plastic cup in hand.

Rain Rain, Wind Wind, Clink Clink, Brrrr!
Edinburgh summer, shelter from a sudden showerrrr.
Flyer distributers and magazine contributors
Here Here, There There, welcoming visitors

Read Read, Listen Listen, Clink Clink, Yes!
Authors and performing acts are invited guests.
Meet a happy reveller, new best forever friend,
Hello Hello, Farewell, Farewell, strangers again.

Late Late, Night Night, Clink Clink, Yawn!
The excitement has ended, we partied from dusk till dawn
Fireworks, music, dart and flow in a darkened sky
Next Year, Next Beer, the Fringe bids us goodbye.

Strange Street
A Novel Extract
W.T.Sutherland

Adam and Paul, as always on a Friday night, were having an evening out in one of the local discos. The lads had been pals since school days; both were in their early twenties but after school although still friends they had each taken different paths in life. Paul had become an apprentice engineer and was now fully qualified in aero engineering, whereas Adam had taken the university route and was about to take his honours exams in chemistry. They had thoroughly enjoyed their evening dancing with the local girls and being with friends until the small hours of the morning. When they left the disco it was very late and once outside they discovered that it was windy and raining heavily. They trudged through the storm but as they progressed they began to notice that sky was changing colour. The black clouds were becoming strange shades of purple, varying in shade in waves across the sky.

To make matters worse thunder and lightning began to illuminate the wet streets in unusual and weird colours. The two lads were completely soaked as they ran along although they were still a good way from their homes. Suddenly they were struck by a freak bolt of violet lightening. That was the last conscience moment as both young men collapsed where they were.

The sun was shining when they came to their senses. They were sprawled out on the pavement and they had no idea how long they had been lying there. Thankfully the street was now dry. They slowly rose shakily to their feet feeling groggy and disorientated. They looked around trying to recognise where they were.

"What hit us? Where are we? "Paul asked. "Do you know this place?"

Adam sat down on a nearby wall; he was shaking and feeling dreadful with a very severe headache. He looked at Paul but took some time before he replied. "I feel bloody awful, I think this is Canal Street but it looks different?" he said.

"I know how you feel. I feel like shit but where are we? I don't recognise anything here." Paul was totally disorientated and looking round desperately trying to recognise where he was.

"Neither do I. Which way were we walking during the storm, any idea?" asked Adam.

"None at all. Maybe we should start walking again then we might recognise something as we go along."

They slowly started walking until they begin to feel stronger. They crossed the road and looked at the name of the street they were in and realised they were in Speygate. That made them feel more comfortable and they began to get their bearings. They recognised some of the buildings but some of them looked strange. They could see to the right that they were near a bridge which they recognised as the bridge over the river Tay.

"Right, this is South Street that is our way home." Adam pointed to the adjacent street. "Oh hell we must have been walking the wrong way we'll have to go back down to Princes Street." Glancing round he said "I haven't been down this way for a while but it certainly looks different."

They continued with a feeling of relief back down past Canal Street but when they walked down they did not recognise this as the street they had known all their lives. As they continued walking they realised that there were a lot of alleyways they had not noticed before. They looked down a long and narrow lane. The buildings on either side were tall and when they looked up it seemed as if the tops of the structures seemed to meet. At intervals there were small and narrow windows which appeared to be more wood frame than glass.

"How did this get here?" asked Paul.

"I've no idea," responded Adam, "we just came down here but I've never seen this place before." As he spoke he turned round to look at the road they had just walked and had to look again. "Wait a minute, I don't know this street! Everything has changed!"

Paul was looking round shocked. How had they found themselves in this strange street.

"Adam, this is crazy. I don't recognise anything about this place. Come on, let's go back to Princes Street." He was really concerned that they were lost in an unfamiliar alleyway and more than that how they had found themselves in this curious place. They turned and made their way back to the end of the alleyway. As they were reaching the corner Adam breathed a sigh of relief but then he realised the lane they were leaving was being replaced by one of a similar appearance. The two of them stood looking at each other.

"What is going on Adam?" asked Paul "Where are we?"

"I have no idea. When we left that lane we turned into what should have been Princes Street. This is not Princes Street. I don't understand how a street can change. I have never seen these streets before."

"There is someone coming," said Paul "Maybe they can tell us where we are."

An old gentleman walked slowly up to the point where the two were standing. His clothes were dirty and of poor quality. "Excuse me sir we seem to be a bit lost, can you tell us where we are?" enquired Adam.

"Well, this is Princes Street. Where did you want to go?" replied the old man.

"This is Princes Street? But we know Princes Street and it's nothing like this!"

"I don't know what you mean. This is Princes Street, always has been," the man replied with a puzzled look on his face before walking away shaking his head,

Adam and Paul were shocked; they were in a strange place which they had thought they knew very well. Now they were beginning to realise that there was something really wrong and they did not know what it was. Adam voiced the thoughts of them both. "I don't know, I don't understand it, we'll just have to keep walking maybe we'll soon start to recognise something."

The two of them continued down the street looking out for familiar landmarks. The lane turned to the right and, as they navigated the bend, they realised the there was a church in front of them which they recognised.

"There's St Stevens but I don't know the buildings on either side. This is crazy. Let's ask in the church."

They tried the door and found that it was open. Very slowly they walked in and were relieved to see that there was a priest coming towards them.

"Hello,Father, are we glad to see you? What has happened to Princes Street?"

"What do you mean, young man, nothing has happened to the street. It is just as it has always been? There is talk of it being rebuilt after the war," the priest responded.

"What do you mean after the war? What war? We are not at war." Adam was alarmed at the priest's remarks.

"What do you mean? We have thousands in Kitchener's army, fighting in France for your king and country which is where you should be. Why are you not in the army? Most young men of your age have volunteered long ago?"

"What are you talking about? Kitchener's army was during the First World War, nearly a hundred years ago. This is 2009, not 1914."

"I don't know what you are talking about; this is 1915. What is the matter with you?" retorted the priest angrily.

"Father, we don't understand. We live in 2009, we walked along Canal Street and into Princes Street and suddenly we are in 1915. This does not make any sense."

"You are right young man, it does not make any sense and I do not know what you are up to but I think you both should leave now before I call the police." The priest was now showing real anger as he ushered them towards the door. "Do not waste the church's time when we have thousands of wounded troops requiring our help. So please go."

"But Father, you do not understand," pleaded Paul, "what Adam said is true, we were brought up in the twenty first century and we are frightened. We do not know what has happened to us."

"I think it is a doctor you need to see. Now go please." The priest was not prepared to help them as he ushered them out of the church.

Once outside Paul was showing his fear and anger "What the hell is happening, Adam? This is nuts."

"There has to be an explanation, I'll try and phone Jimmy and see what he has to say."

As he spoke Adam took out his mobile phone and dialled a number. He waited for a moment then turned to Paul and said, "Nothing! There is not even a dialling tone, nothing at all."

Adam and Paul were now beginning to worry about their situation. They did not recognise the street they were in and they had just been told by the priest that the country was in the middle of the First World War. They continued walking. Everything appeared different but there was enough for them to recognise where they were. They found a park bench and sat down to review their position.

"What happened last night?" asked Paul. He answered himself saying, "We left the club and started to walk home when the storm started, then the sky was turned purple and I think we were hit by lightning."

"Yes, that's what I think as well but when we came to everything seemed to have changed," Adam responded. "Either that or we have been brought back in time?"

"You're joking. How could that happen?" Paul had not been prepared to consider this answer.

"I don't how but that's what I think has happened. I think that somehow we are in 1915 as the priest said," Adam replied.

"OK, just suppose you are right, how do we get back?

"I have no idea. How did we get here? I don't know what it was that brought us back to this time but I wish we knew then we might be able to reverse it."

"One thing I notice; there are not too many people around. What time is it?"

Adam looked at his watch. "Ten to one, that can't be right. What time do you make it? My watch seems to have stopped."

Paul looked at his watch "Mine's the same. Ten to one. They must have stopped when the storm struck."

"Well at least we know what time we have been sent back to, even if we don't know how."

"Well I wonder how long were we out. It was light when we came to, so it must still be early. Maybe we'll see more people as time goes on."

They rose and started walking again though they had no idea in which direction. They walked for about half a mile and came upon a school with children in the playground.

"Well, it's at least nine o'clock if the kids are in school so at least we know that much."

As they walked past the children crowded at the railing staring at the two men who, to them, were dressed in a funny way. Paul and Adam were a puzzle to them as the clothes the two were wearing, as far as the youngsters were concerned, were very strange.

The childrens' cries and the fact that they were clustered at the railing drew the attention of one of the teachers who came over to investigate.

"Who are you, why are you waiting here at the fence? I think you should move on," he said

I'm sorry sir but we are lost. Could you tell us where we are?"

"You are in Perth and this is Links School. Now, please move away," replied the harassed teacher.

"Thank you," said Adam as he tugged on Paul's sleeve to get him to leave.

Once away from the school fence he said, "Paul this situation is crazy. We will have to take care; people don't understand who we are. If the reaction of the others is how people see us then we will have to be careful. We could be mistaken for German spies. If we have gone back in time and it is 1915 then there is a war on!"

Adam was becoming worried for their safety.

"What can we do Adam? How do we get back to 2009?"

"I have no idea but I think we should get out of this area."

They walked further on where there were more pedestrians who seemed to give them curious looks. They came to a small shop. As they turned the corner at the side of the shop they found a young girl sitting on the window ledge sobbing quietly.

As no other people seemed to have paid her any attention they stopped, noting that she had bright modern style clothes.

"Are you alright?" asked Paul.

The girl looked at the two lads for a moment before answering. "I'm frightened; I don't know where I am."

"You are still in Perth. Were you in a thunder storm last night?" responded Adam.

"Yes, I was knocked out but when I recovered everything was different," the frightened girl replied.

"That is because this is 1915 not 2009 and the First World War is on. We were caught in the same storm. I think we should stick together. What is your name?" asked Adam.

"Louise. Louise Ross," replied the frightened girl, though now relieved that someone understood how she was feeling.

"Hi, Louise, I'm Paul Smith and this is Adam Collins. We were at a disco in Robertson Crescent. When we left we were struck by some sort of funny lightning."

"I was there too. I had just left the building when I was hit. I have no idea how long I was out. When I woke up I did not recognise where I was and just started to walk. I kept getting funny looks from people but they are strange." As she spoke it was obvious that she was still very upset.

"Why don't you come with us? At least we understand each other. There may be more like us around here, feeling just as we do," suggested Adam

"Were you alone when you were hit by the lightning?"

"Yes, I left alone before my friends as I had just fallen out with my boyfriend then bang and I woke up alone," Louise declared.

"So, you must have been at the door as we were leaving the street. Were there any other people around as you left? inquired Paul

"I can't remember. I would imagine there were. I left after the club closed so I would think that other people would be leaving about that time," she observed.

"I wonder where they are? The chances are they were struck too. Did you see any others when you came to?" Adam asked

"There were some people near me but I don't know if they were hit by the lightning. I was so confused I really don't know."

"Right, I would suggest that you stick with us. We're all in the same boat and there are probably more. We have to find a way to get back to 2009. I know it's crazy but we are out of our time."

As the two boys, now accompanied by Louise, started walking, a young woman came out of a side street weeping profusely. Paul was nearest to her.

"Are you alright? Can we help you, dear," he enquired.

"My husband, he's dead," she cried. "He's dead, they killed him."

"Who killed him?" asked Adam, very shocked.

"They did, the army. He was sent to France last week and now he is dead."

Louise came forward to comfort the distraught young woman, putting her arm round her and walking with her along the street. "Where do you stay? You should be at home with your family at this time," she said.

"I live round the corner. When I got the telegram I went to my mother's house in Green Street, I tried not to let her see how upset I was. We have only been married six months." She paused then looking round through her tears at the trio before saying, "Who are you? You look different, where are you from? You speak very good English."

Louise looked at Adam and Paul before she answered. "We come from up north. We are just down here visiting."

"Oh I see, I'm sorry, I did not mean to be rude."

"Don't worry, dear, but I think you should talk to your mother though. I'm sure she will understand," suggested Louise.

"You don't know my mother. She will tell me not to be so sentimental, and she will say that I've got to be strong." The young girl was obviously torn between grief and a desire to please her mother.

Adam and Paul were becoming a little impatient with the situation,. "I think we should get on, Louise, we really should try to get home."

Both Louise and Adam knew what he meant.

"I'm sorry I'm keeping you back. Thank you." The young girl turned back to the street she had left.

"I think you should talk to your Mum, dear, I'm sure she will understand," said Louise as she gave the young woman a hug.

They left as the young girl still sobbing slowly walked back the way she had come while they continued walking along the road, though they had no idea where they were walking.

"We don't know what it feels like to be at war. That poor woman was absolutely distraught," stated Paul.

The three continued along away from the street that the woman had entered.

This incident had brought home to them some idea of what it was like being at war. They had no experience of the terrible tragedy of family and friends losing their lives in warfare.

When they reached the next corner they were met by four people, two boys and two girls, walking towards them. Judging by their dress they were from the same era as themselves. Both parties looked at each other for a moment then, "Hello, you look as if you do not belong here. Were you caught in a thunderstorm by any chance?" asked Paul

"Yes. Were you?" replied the spokesman.

"Yes and we seem to be in another time zone. My name's Paul and this is Adam and Louise," he said indicating the young lady in question. "And the date is 1915."

"Did you say 1915? It can't be, this is 2009, is it not? I'm John and this is my girlfriend, June, my pal Ian and this is Susan," he said indicating each one in turn.

"Well, I think it would be a good thing if we stick together.. From what we've been told this is 1915 and we are in the middle of the First World War," stated Paul.

"What! But we can't just go back in time like that, it doesn't make sense. What is the name of this place?" Ian, the second newcomer exclaimed.

"This is Perth and the main thing I recognise is the river, that's the Tay, but I don't know what has happened to the town. Some parts are familiar but there is a lot of it different. The thing is how do we get back to 2009?

"I don't think we need to worry about that. Look, we have company?" Adam announced. The group turned to look along the street as two policemen were approaching them. The two policemen were dressed in a manner that Paul had seen in books with long tunics buttoned to the neck and the same kind of helmets they still wore in some of the English police forces.

"What are you people doing? Have you been to a fancy dress party or something?" asked the first policemen.

"No we are lost, we are from Perth but, through no fault of our own, we seem to be in a different time."

"What are you talking about? Why are you not in the army fighting for the King and country? Are you conscientious objectors?" was the response.

"No, he told you, we are from 2009 and we find ourselves here. We live in Perth but not at this time. We are not lying, we are afraid. We do not understand this any more than you do." Louise was pleading and fear was noticeable in her voice.

"I think you are off your heads but you better come with us to the police station," said the second policeman who up till now had said nothing but had been watching them closely.

"If you can help us to get back to 2009 we will be glad to go anywhere with you," responded Adam while the two coppers exchanged glances with raised eyebrows,

"Yes, we'll see what we can do. If you have a map we'll be delighted to help you to get to where you want to go."

The group proceeded to make their way to the police station which was a few streets away. To local people seeing this procession it looked as if the police had caught some prisoners who were all dressed in funny clothes. John and his three companions were walking at the rear of the group. Suddenly they decided to run. The four of them made for the corner of the street they had just passed and disappeared from view within seconds. As there were only two policemen they could only note their exit but they were concentrating on getting Paul Adam and Louise to the police station as quickly as possible.

The duty officer at the desk was constable McGowan who looked up in surprise when they walked into the entrance of the office and when he heard about the story being told by the trio he was very sceptical how anybody could come from a later time. It made no sense, they were just dressed funny.

"Is it possible that we could have something to eat and drink, we have had nothing since we arrived at this time," asked Louise.

"Why don't you go home then? Where do you stay?" responded McGowan.

"South Inch Quadrant," replied Louise.

"That's ridiculous, there are no house at the South Inch. It is open space. Where do you live?" persisted the constable.

"I've told you, South Inch Quadrant. The house was built in the 1930s," asserted Louise. "That is what we are talking about, we live in the year 2009, will no one believe us?"

"What do you want us to believe, young lady, and why are you all here dressed like that?" The question came from an older man who had entered the office.

"This is inspector McNeish," announced McGowan.

"What's this rabble all about, constable?" the inspector enquired.

"These people say they are from the year 2009 sir. I think they must be on some sort of drug."

"Can we have something to eat and drink? None of us have been able to have anything since we arrived," Louise again asked.

"Arrived? Where have you come from?" McNeish asked.

"We've told you we live in Perth but in the year 2009." Adam replied.

"Right, bring them into one of the interview rooms, constable. Let's see what they are on and where they got the stuff," announced McLeish

"What about that cup of tea and some food," pleaded Louise?

"All in good time young lady, now move," he insisted, opening the door at the back of the office and ushering them all through.

The three from another time were ushered into a large room and two policemen moved in with extra chairs.

The inspector sat down at a table and opened the questioning. "Right, we have had enough of this nonsense. Where are you from and what have you all been up to?"

"We have told you the truth, Inspector; we have no more idea of what has happened to us than you. We were having a night out and when we came outside there was a thunder storm. I don't know about the others but I think I was hit by lightning and when I came to I was here." He paused. "A hundred years back in time."

"This is getting ridiculous. Put them in the cells and get the duty doctor. These people are on something and I want to know what and where they are getting it."

"We are not on anything. Don't you recognise the truth when you hear it?" shouted Adam. "We are only wanting to get back to our own time. Can you help us or is your only answer to lock us up?"

McNeish ignored the comments and nodded to the constable, indicating that he wanted the group in a cell.

Seline's Family Tree
Eric McFarlane

"Can I help you?" said the nice man at the bookshop door with the green tie.

I gave him my soaking umbrella to hold while I carried on looking at the magazines.

I had just popped into the book shop to get out of the rain, so that's why I was stood standing at the magazines. I wasn't going to buy anything, I mean they're all so expensive - pounds they cost, most of them. I remember when you could get the People's Friend for 6d, mind I couldn't afford it then either. You can buy magazines on anything these days. Senga, she's my best friend, bought one the other day that was just about a field in Scotland. I don't know how you can write a magazine about a field. Anyway I had a look through one or two just so I wouldn't look too odd while I was waiting for the rain to go off.

I picked up *Gay Gardener* because I like flowers and gardening and stuff like that but it was a little strange.

"Excuse me." It was the man with the green tie. He was looking embarrassed. "I think this is your umbrella," he said.

I took a close look at it. "Yes, that's mine," I said. It's quite easy to tell on account of it's purple with a lion on and a broken spoke.

"I think you should take it back," he said.

"Yes of course," I said. "I'll get it just as soon as I leave. You just wait over by the door."

I put the *Gay Gardener* back, I didn't understand it. It was then I saw the magazine beside it - *Gentle Genealogy vol1 no1* it called itself, and underneath *Genealogy for the fainthearted*. Actually, at first I thought it said farted rather than fainthearted. You know how sometimes you read words that aren't really there, it can be quite embarrassing. I had to read it several times. I think fainthearted made more sense. I knew what Genealogy was, I saw a programme on telly about it, and it just suddenly came to me what Mam used to say about our family, only I've forgot what it was right now, but anyway when she said it I remember thinking that surely they couldn't have been as bad as that.

I started reading the introduction in the magazine and it told about how easy it was to find out about all your famous ancestors. I got to thinking how I might be related to the Queen or even that Barbara Dickson with the voice.

"Excuse *me*." It was that man with the silly tie. He was waving my umbrella around and looking quite agitated. He was obviously not right in the head. "I am not an umbrella stand," he says.

I stared at him. Well what can you say? I mean he looked perfectly normal. I didn't want to antagonise him, him not having quite enough fat in the pan, as Mam used to say.

"No, no indeed you're not," I said. I smiled at him to try and make him feel relaxed but it didn't work. His face went quite red. Normally I would have given him a talk about customer service but this was not the moment.

"Look, I'm just going to buy this magazine right over here by the door where that nice lady takes the money. Then I'll collect my umbrella from you, even though you are not an umbrella stand, and you can go back to being whatever you are, which will be nice now, won't it?"

His eyes had gone all bulgy and his nostrils were flared out like he was breathing really, really hard. He didn't say anything more but marched over to the door holding my umbrella between his finger tips. A tall man in a bow tie talked to him. He waved his arms about but then he seemed to calm down after that.

I joined the queue to pay for my magazine. The tie man was standing near the door with his eyes shut, sort of rocking backwards and forwards gently and I realised that he really looked sort of, you know... nice. He was a wee bit taller than me and maybe a bit older but he had all his hair and looked very smart in his shiny shoes. OK perhaps he was a bit short upstairs but at least he could tie his shoelaces. Right, Seline, I thought, use your willies. That's what Mam used to tell me, if you want to get your man, Seline, you've got to use your feminine willies. I tipped my hat slightly sideways and undid the top button of my raincoat. It didn't seem much so I undid another button and pulled out the collar of my cardie. Well it would have to do for the moment. The lady behind the till was staring at me peculiarly.

"It's not for you, dear," I said and gave her a big wink. I think she got the message, she served me really quickly.

I sauntered over to the man by the door, who still seemed to have his eyes shut. I stood beside him for a second and then I leant over and said in his ear. "You can give it me now. I'm ready."

He jumped backwards and let out this funny sort of gurgling noise and dropped my brolly right at my feet which really was a bit silly considering he'd been holding it all this time. He was lying back against the wall with his hand on his chest just sort of staring at me and making these strange noises. He really was a most peculiar man, too peculiar for me, I decided. I picked up my brolly, thanked him and left.

The rain had stopped so I decided to walk home. An ambulance came screeching round the corner a few minutes later making an awful racket.

I told Senga about it when I got home. "Trust you to fall for an umbrella stand, love," was all she said. I don't think she quite understood what I was saying

"What do you think about genealogy, Senga," I said.

"If it keeps you out of mischief, Seline, I'm all for it," she said.

Train To Waverley
Ian Macartney

The landscape runs away from the window.
Still lakes and nets over rock and
forests never walked and
sometimes cracked wall and
a weed city flourishing,
only seen through the glass.

A Mac lets a list
jump down in the reflection, while later
a long text spreads syntax to claim crystal.
Opposite, a teenage man furrows at his phone
with golden glasses and near-red headphones.

(Im)pale fence to sulphur-yellow bush:
heritage peach to grey
clan-squares proclaiming
arches needing cleaned
and doors the colour
of wet washing,
older even than the swings and
sleeping play parks in gardens not too lost.

Haymarket stops.
A floating island of glass panels
telling the time to the nearest second
and coffee shops and suitcases and suits,
a cloud city hovering over the rails.
Fans eager to meet their destination
gather at the edge.

A tunnel comes like a stormcloud,
cosy charcoal.
The other diesel horse is
transparent in speed,
illuminating the brick.
A lamp with life
in a human coloured light.
It alleviates the void's question mark.

Out, light, and a
garden of immigrant grasses
mingles with unplaced track.

Waverley stops sprinting
and catches a breath.

Quiet Sunday
Chris Gorman

It was a typical quiet spring Sunday afternoon. As I drove my bus up Leith Walk I was conscious of the fact that I was running a bit early. I had to be careful not to get caught out by one of the inspectors, who would tear me off a strip if I arrived at or left from one of the checkpoints ahead of the scheduled time.

What were you supposed to do when it was quiet like this? I thought, *crawl along at a snail's pace?*

The fact of the matter was that, if you did just that, the customers would all be wondering if there was a mechanical problem with the bus. A few would even ask if that was the case.

When I got to the top of Leith Walk I sat for a while at the bus stop. This of course resulted in questions about "what was the matter? Has the bus broken down? When are we getting underway?" etc. Eventually I pulled out and slowly made my way to the junction of East Princes Street and Waverly Bridge and arrived exactly at the appointed time. In fact there was no inspector there, but there was a policeman. He was on traffic duty and he signalled me to stop.

Ah, that's fine, I thought. *Natural delays are better than crawling or waiting for the clock to catch up.*

What was that ahead? I took off my glasses and rubbed my eyes before returning them to my face. I looked again. If I didn't know any better I could swear that was an elephant's arse I could see ahead of me.

I glanced to my left where I could see the policeman beckoning to the traffic coming up Waverly Bridge and turning into Princes Street. Traffic! What I now witnessed were five Indian elephants walking up the street and turning left to join their brother whose was just ahead of them. Alongside each beast walked a man dressed in a turban and Tunic.

I almost burst out laughing. *Well, this will certainly slow my pace.* When the last of the six elephants had turned into Princes Street, the policeman, who was now joined by a colleague, signalled to me to proceed. The two policemen now walked at a slow pace a few yards behind the last of the animals and indicated to the traffic that we should not get too close. By now there was quite a cue of vehicles behind me but we had no choice but to drive at elephant walking speed. Now, Princes Street is approximately one mile long. When we reached the west end we proceeded, still following our fellow creatures, in a western direction until we came to Haymarket. By now my bus was twenty minutes behind schedule but I was in a cheery mood. I had enjoyed the site of the people lining the route we had just taken. Cheering, flag waving and the expression on the faces (especially those of the children} was a sight to see. At this point the police made a special arrangement for the traffic to pass and so we proceeded on our way.

As I approached the first bus stop after the Haymarket I spotted, right at the head of the queue, a 'Corstorphinite'. For the uninitiated, a 'Corstorphinite' is a resident of the village of Corstorphine who is usually an elderly lady carrying a walking stick or an umbrella and ready to complain, moan and otherwise piss everybody off at the drop of a hat. Many refer to this type as 'fur coat and nae knickers'. As soon as I opened the door she started.

"Where have you been? I've been waiting ages for this bus," she yelled as she showed me her bus pass.

"I'm very sorry madam but we got stuck behind six elephants walking along Princess Street."

"Don't give me any of your impertinence, young man," she exclaimed, shaking her folded umbrella as if it was some kind of weapon. "That kind of sarcasm doesn't impress me."

"I'm telling you, madam. There were six elephants walking along Princes Street and the police wouldn't allow us to pass until we got to Haymarket."

"That does it. I am going to report you for your rudeness. I will write to your bosses in the strongest possible terms. Just let me get a note of your number."

And she started routing around in her handbag for a pen. Just at that point I noticed that an inspector had been edging his way to the front of a rather disgruntled crowd who were getting even more annoyed at the amount of time this woman was taking to get on the bus. The inspector mounted the bus.

"No need to bother writing in madam," I said, "Here's a gentleman who can deal with your complaint."

"I was just asking this driver about the reason for this bus being late," she started up in a shrieking tone, "and he gives me nonsense about elephants in Princes Street. He seems to think that because I'm elderly he can fire cheeky answers at me."

"I'm sorry," said the inspector, "but I'm afraid the driver is correct. I've just had a call on my radio from my control room. Just half an hour ago six Indian elephants arrived in Edinburgh on board a train that came into Waverly station and as their final destination was Murrayfield they had to complete the journey by road. So they decided to turn it into a little parade. Madam, it gives me great pleasure to announce that the circus has come to town."

The Stalker
Elizabeth Hands

He stood leaning on the bus stop, looking as though he was waiting for a bus. But he was not. Jean knew he was not. She knew he was watching her.

Trying not to be seen, she watched him for a while then decided to take action. She moved from her hiding place to her kitchen table. Lifting the pen, she began to write a detailed description of him: white, age around late 20s, approximately 5' 8'', dark hair with receding hair line at front – when the phone rang.

She jumped. Who could be calling? She'd phoned in sick to her work and her only sister was in Spain on holiday. Getting up to answer the insistent ringing, she moved to her viewpoint to see if he was using his phone. As far as she could make out he was not, so she picked up the phone. When she heard his voice saying hello, the phone fell from her hand and she stood transfixed.

How could he be phoning? She'd checked. Perhaps he had one of those phones which fitted into his ear? Perhaps …

She stopped thinking and shaking as she heard the tone signalling that he had hung up. How could a simple hello provoke such a strong reaction?

She began to cry with anger, frustration and fear. What had she done to deserve this? Stop it, she scolded herself, and moved back to the table with the phone. She picked up the pen and this time decided to write out the whole story in case the police needed it. She was sure this would come to a sticky end.

Of one thing she was certain: he wanted to kill her and would succeed. She wanted to at least put up some kind of fight even if it was from the grave.

She re-read her account and noticed she had neither the name of the coffee shop nor Charlie's surname so she added these. Then she laughed; a nervous laugh. You idiot, she chided herself, the police would find out the details. Again she laughed.

Going back to her vantage point near the window, she saw he was still there, still staring up at her window.

She sat back down and tried to remember all the other 'chance' meetings over the months. He has never spoken, except twice said hello on the phone, but has always made his presence felt.

I am being stalked, she finally admitted.

Hearing herself say it out loud helped strengthen her resolve. Calm yourself, she chided herself again. Get on with your report for the police. I wonder how many victims leave clues like this?

Over the next couple of hours she listed times and events to the best of her memory. She hoped they were accurate, because it had taken several encounters for her to realise that she kept bumping into this young man at different times and days of the week in a variety of places. She explained all of this in her report.

By now her report was several pages long. When she re-read it she felt it read like a neurotic middle-aged spinster making mountains out of molehills. She didn't care. It was vital to give as much factual information as possible to help the police find witnesses to the encounters which would enable them to build up a case against him.

Good God women you've changed from a person into a case, she thought. Stop being so negative, you're not dead yet. As she said this aloud, she could not but think that her original thoughts about her impending end were undeniable.

She rose from the table and switched on the kettle. I have to do something about him, she thought, while she prepared her evening meal. Perhaps I should go out and confront him. Or call the Police now? Perhaps …….

Her intentions were cut short by the door bell ringing. She made her way to the door, then stopped dead. What if it's him? Should I get a knife for protection? Should I call the police? Should I pretend I'm not at home?

The bell rang again as she walked over to her vantage point at the window. He was no longer at the bus stop. She moved back to the table and picked up her report. Opening the kitchen cupboard, she slipped her report into the box of cornflakes for the police to find. With the box replaced in the cupboard, she went quietly into the hall. As she reached the door, the bell rang for the third time.

Without further hesitation she opened the door and there stood the man she so dreaded. He looked younger and somehow less frightening than before.

'Can I help you?' she asked, her voice surprisingly firm.

Time seemed to stop as Jean waited for him to speak or act. When he did, his reply overwhelmed her:

"I hope so. I think you might be my birth mother."

"...we spend our years as a tale that is told."
Psalm 90 verse 9 KJV
Anne E. Edwards

We were as two bookends,
the facts and fictions of our lives held fast between us.
Sometimes I forget,
then coming home I remember.
We call birth an everyday miracle,
and death too is an everyday event.
Like birth,
the mother forgets the pain of labour.
Like death,
the pain dulls as we move on.
The mother kisses the new babies head,
a baptism of gratefulness,
brim-full of the warmth of life.
We kiss the forehead of the newly extinguished,
amazed at how cold and lifeless they have become,
surprised at no response.
A cry, a stretch, a cough,
we grow in seasons,
like corn in the night,
to pop and crackle in the sun
held in a warm palm
still and solid for a moment
then flung into the void

The Musical Rabbit

Margaret Walker

My parents died within weeks of one another. They had been fairly healthy for their age but the Grim Reaper can never be beaten. They were never away from the local community centre – tea dancing, line dancing, any sort of dancing really (well, maybe not disco). Dad sang in the church choir. Mother, who had been a piano teacher for most of her life, still played her music – Beethoven sonatas, Chopin, Schumann. But no matter how much they danced and sang and played music the inevitable happened, though not till their late eighties.

As the only daughter it fell to me to make all the necessary arrangements. Mother's relatives came through from Ayr. Father's relations from Aberdeen, however, could not manage and sent flowers. Months passed in a whirlwind of visits, cards, hugs, tears and reminiscences. Then came quieter weeks when I sat alone in their house carefully going through their things. And what mountains of stuff they had collected! All of it was dear to them but not of much value to me.

They had moved house a lot so any trace of me or my brother had long since been cleared out, to jumble sales or to the bin. My brother had died young in a road accident; it was the biggest loss imaginable for them and for me. All they had left of his life was a large framed photograph of his Graduation Day; a serious-looking boy with gold-rimmed spectacles and a beard, holding his white scroll from Glasgow University, wearing the loaned-out graduation gown, fixed forever in his youth. The photo was faded but I would keep it.

Other things I cleared out into boxes and bags to go to charity shops. Piles of clothes, books, records, pictures, videos, DVDs. I kept a few of the latter: how they had loved Alistair Sim, a dry-witted Scotsman of Ealing film studios vintage. Their favourite film of all was a comedy called "The Green Man" in which Alistair Sim plays an assassin and his accomplice-in-crime has to murder a middle-aged lady called Marigold who has guessed his secret. After killing her (as he thinks) the accomplice hides her body in a grand piano.

"He put her inside a piano!" exclaims Sim, aghast, as though the act of murder is perfectly acceptable: the unforgivable crime is to hide the victim in a musical instrument. My parents always hooted with laughter at this bit and mum's eyes would glance towards her own piano which would never, in her mind, have to undergo such an indignity.

Amongst the clearing-out I came upon a very old toy, a rabbit wearing a blue coat. The base of the rabbit was a musical-box covered with a pink velvet skirt. She had a small label bearing the name "Chiltern" a long-gone English toy manufacturer. I wound it up, it still worked and Brahms' Lullaby tinkled from beneath the faded pink skirt. As I listened I suddenly became seven years old again. The annual pilgrimage to Glasgow to do our Christmas shopping and admire the displays of lights strung across the busy streets. Above the din of traffic came an even louder sound – starlings roosting on the buildings in the deepening dusk, squawking and chattering. I do not know if that still happens or not: I suspect not, at least in such vast numbers.

"I want that rabbit!" I cried.

My parents checked the price: "No, this is far too expensive, you can have a game or something else," they explained. But nothing else would do and I sulked in the train all the way back to Ayr. Then, on Christmas morning – joy! – I had the musical rabbit among my pile of gifts. And here she was now, a living memory of family Christmases: granny through to stay for the week, roaring coal fires, turkey and delicious plum puddings. Talk about buried treasure! I carefully wrapped the rabbit in bubble-wrap and tissue paper and placed her in a shoe-box.

My cousins came from Ayr and took away all the bags and boxes, it was too heavy for me but they distributed the stuff amongst various charity shops and second-hand traders.

A while later, I looked for the shoe-box and the rabbit but I could not find it. I searched everywhere but it had gone! How could this have happened? I felt the loss keenly. The grief for the lost toy was way out of proportion to the thing itself. I phoned or visited all the charity shops I could, but nothing. Maybe it had been sold on: no-one could remember seeing it, the shop assistants shrugged. Perhaps rough hands had thrown the shabby article into a bin. The little toy seemed to represent all my loved ones – gran, parents, brother, much-loved pets, old lost toys – all vanished as though into a black hole, all gone forever.   How could something so irreplaceable have vanished? The extent of my losses only really hit me then and I cried bitterly. But then, perhaps that was life: love then loss, over and over.

I tried to keep myself busy. That was of some help. In time, I decided I would rent out my parents' house including their furniture. I had never been a landlord before so I had much to learn.

There was a flood of interest; rented properties in that area were like gold. The cousins came through again, perhaps they thought I was not capable of doing business. They settled on a nice Polish family. . The mother worked as a cleaner and the father was a builder. They had fallen in love with the house and offered all sorts of plans for improvements which they were happy to do. To be sure, the work badly needed doing and I could afford to take a slightly lower rent in return.

My own choice however was quite different. A serious-looking young man of twenty-three called Michael had answered the advertisement. He worked on his own as a piano teacher and he was finding it impossible to get a mortgage. Something about him reminded me of my brother, the same age and the same open, steady gaze. I decided mother would be pleased to rent her house to a piano teacher and we signed the lease there and then. Michael was delighted to hear that I planned to include mother's piano with the furniture: I did not play and had no use for it. The cousins were horrified – "A single guy! He'll be having wild parties!" But I didn't think so. And it would be nice to have children in the house again getting music lessons.

Not long after he moved in I went round to do some work in the garden. The plants were a link to my parents: mum's favourite roses and dad's carefully pruned shrubs. As I hoed and weeded and watered a familiar car drew up on the driveway. Its door opened and a pleasant looking man got ou carrying a heavy bag. He did not see me at first and rang the bell. Michael answered the door and as the man was about to go in he caught sight of me.

"Oh, I am so sorry," he exclaimed, putting the big bag down. "How are you? I heard about your mum and dad" and he came over and gave me a big bear-hug.

"Thank you Robert," I smiled. "Well, I am fine, but I take it the piano needs tuning."

"Indeed it does."

Michael had come out. "Come in when you are finished and I'll make some tea," he said to me, and he followed Robert in to the house.

I had soon tidied up, put away the gardening stuff and went in to the house. In the lounge I could hear Robert and Michael laughing heartily. "No wonder it sounded so bad!" I heard Michael say. Curious, I followed the voices.

"Look here, someone's been playing a joke on you," smiled Robert when he saw me. "This was inside the piano." And he held out a shoe-box.

"Oh my God!" I gasped, scarcely daring to believe my eyes. I took the box, opened it, and there she lay, my darling old musical rabbit.

Outdoor Gallery
Sally Thomson

For two weeks in May
Our street becomes
An outdoor gallery
Abstract art on full display

Smears and splats
Dried dribbles of mixed hues
Yellow, green, white
Black and grey

No object escapes
Cars, windows, tarmac,
Walls, fence, foliage
Fresh clean sheets
Drying in the sun

All covered with graffiti
From these fleeting artists
Determined to leave their mark

Jet washing cars
Doesn't stop their goal
New art, for all to see
Swiftly appearing
On the now gleaming car

Constant chatter
Background chorus
Interrupted with song

And high-pitched whistles
Flight paths above
Full of small dark feathers
Dangling worms

A Way Out
Norman Geddes

Ben Winston felt out of place and the feeling was not new. The others were young and vigorous with trendy suits and film star hairstyles. Ben was pushing sixty and weary of the whole business. He slouched in a suit which aged him more accurately than the grey of his hair or anything else about him. He owned better suits but refused to wear them to work. It was a small token of rebellion.

Eight sales representatives were cramped into Colin Rice's small office for the weekly meeting. There were seats for only five so Ben, having been last to arrive, leaned against a steel filing cabinet like a hastily dumped roll of carpet. Eight graphs on one wall traced their sales figures and the line on Ben's graph was progressing steadily towards the floor. It had not always been so.

Ben glanced at his colleagues noting the rapt attention on each face as they listened to their keen young sales manager. Colin Rice had come, newly promoted, with the recent take-over; twenty six years old and impatient to soar.

'I came here,' Rice was saying in his now familiar rhetoric, to revitalise the sales team and spearhead a new, aggressive offensive in the field. My first six months have been praised from on high (he pointed at the ceiling) but, personally, I am disappointed. We are not realising our full potential.'

Ben's sigh was audible. Rice shot him a stare that would have turned Niagara Falls into an ice sculpture. He then resumed. 'Some of you have responded quite promisingly to the new initiative. Others ... ' He paused theatrically for effect, '... seem to think they are still employed by the same tired old firm, now defunct and replaced by Wilson Hastings Ltd. I am here to remind these people otherwise, to propel them into our brave new world, to urge them to charge onwards with the rest of us or get off the bus at the next stop because we don't carry passengers.'

As Rice leaned back in his chair looking very chuffed with himself, Ben repressed a snort of laughter with great difficulty. But Rice was moving on. 'Get out there and sell! Sell yourselves, sell your company and sell your products. Remember, there is a vast difference between a salesman and an order collector.' He looked at Ben, perhaps to strike home the point where it most applied; perhaps just to erase the smirk.

When the meeting finally broke up Ben was asked to remain behind. Rice did not resume his chair but perched himself on the edge of his desk with a calculated air of chummy informality. Ben sat on one of the newly vacated chairs.

'You've been at this game a long time, Ben, eh?'

'Thirty three years.'

'Same company all that time?'

Ben nodded. 'Until you lot took over. I did good business and I got it without any of this high pressure stuff. I did business by winning the respect and loyalty of my customers and I won that by giving good, personal service.'

Rice treated him to a sad little smile. 'Times change, Ben. Your old firm couldn't keep up and that's why they had to sell out to us. Now if we were to carry on trading as they did … well … we'd go out of business too.'

Ben said nothing.

'You're not too old to change. The younger lads haven't found it any easier than you. They have youth on their side but you have experience … thirty three years of it. All it needs is commitment and application.'

As he drove home in the company owned Ford Cortina, Ben considered his situation for the umpteenth time. It had always seemed to him that Rice's words of encouragement were delivered with exactly the opposite intention. Telling a sixty year old salesman that he could change into a high power whiz kid was like telling a bus driver that, with a little application, he could captain an ocean going liner. What Rice was really saying was 'change or go'.

Pringle's Model shop came back into Ben's mind as he drove. They needed an assistant and Ben knew and loved their business. A model railway enthusiast, he had been a customer of Pringle's since he'd been a lad. John Pringle Jnr had jokingly offered him the job a few days ago and had been surprised by Ben's semi-serious interest.

'I'd take you on in a minute, Ben, and you know that fine. Only, there's not much money in it and no Ford Cortina.'

Ben had started thinking seriously about it. The money wasn't that important. He and Alice weren't rich but neither were they hard up and their mortgage was paid off. With a little care they could manage fine on Pringle's wages. The problem was Alice.

'A model shop, Ben?' she had said. 'What would people say?'

'They can say what they like,' was Ben's reaction. He had no time for the petty snobbery of his neighbourhood but he knew that his wife was very much caught up in it and that she believed his job carried a degree of prestige. 'Look at Stan down the road there. He had some fancy bloody job when he moved here but now he wheels barrow loads of dung around a garden centre.'

'Quite so,' Alice acknowledged, 'but he isn't exactly there through choice, is he?'

'No,' Ben responded strongly, 'he's there because he lost his licence through drinking and driving!'

'Exactly,' said Alice. 'He didn't abdicate his position, there was no suggestion that he was a failure. In a similar sort of way John Weatherburn had to give up his directorship with Mitchell's

66

because of his heart attack. He's a solicitors' messenger now.' She paused for a moment then said; 'You might like to try that, Ben. Go to Dr. Sharp and get him to declare you unfit for your present job. Stress, perhaps. Then you could work in your little model shop. People would *understand*.'

'You wouldn't mind if I did that, Alice?'

Alice shook her head. 'But do think hard about it. All I'm saying is that if you are dead set on running away from your present job, that is the way to go about it. We don't want people thinking you're a failure, do we?'

But Ben did not want to go to the doctor and lie about his health. He was proud of his health and would rather be branded a failure than a wreck.

The following Friday, after the weekly sales meeting, he joined his colleagues for a drink in *The Sportsman* lounge just across the road. His arrival was met with surprise because had never been one of *The Sportsman* crowd.

'What's this, Ben, taking to the demon drink?' There was a lot of laughter but it was good natured banter. Ben was well liked by these young men.

'It's the demon Rice I'm after,' he said as he joined them. More laughter. Someone bought him a drink, his first gin and tonic of the evening. There were to be many more and by the time Colin Rice made his appearance Ben, drinking heavily on an empty stomach, was merry to say the least.

Rice grinned and raised his eyebrows. 'Well, well, I never expected to see you here, Ben. Decided to mess with the NCOs, eh?'

'Exactly right, Mr Rice.'

One of the reps, recognised by Ben as a prize crawler, scurried off to fetch Rice a drink, brandy and American dry ginger.

Rice took a seat at the low oblong table. 'Never mind the Mr Rice bit here, Ben. Outside the office, we're all mates together.'

'Oh, I see,' said Ben, smiling broadly. 'OK, sonny boy, here's to you!' And he raised his glass, 'And to your little empire!'

Rice's face took on a rattled expression but he forced a little smile. 'It's *our* empire, Ben, not just mine.'

Ben nodded. 'Quite so,' he said, 'quite so.' He had decided it was not yet time to lunge for the jugular; Rice had not yet had enough to drink. And so he leaned back, sipped his own drink and listened to the conversation between crown prince and toadying minions.

Rice swallowed brandy in large, frequent gulps and no sooner was one glass half empty than another was placed in front of him by another of the faithful. When he judged the time was right, Ben brought him one. 'Beware Greeks bearing gifts,' he said with a grin.

Rice raised the fresh glass. 'Thank you, Ben. Cheers!'

'Cheers,' said Ben, I hope you enjoy it. After I bought it I went to the Gents and peed in it. You'd never know, would you?'

Rice had a mouthful of the brandy and, with eyes staring wildly, looked uncertain whether to swallow or spit. Finally he swallowed. Then he grinned. 'You've got some sense of humour, Ben.'

'That wasn't humour,' said Ben, 'That was wishful thinking. I'd love to piss in your drink, you lousy, conceited little creep.'

The toadies stared down into their drinks and cringed. Ben pressed on. 'You're head's full of figures and targets and shit. You know nothing about winning business through customer care because you don't care about your customers. All you care about is grabbing their money and boosting your own standing as you head for the stars. Put simply, you are a cheap, selfish little bastard.'

And with these words Ben left the stricken assembly. He headed to a public telephone just outside the lounge bar.

'I want to report a drunk driver,' he said, 'and if your quick enough you'll get him before he leaves the car park.'

And so they did. 'We have reason to believe you have been drinking, sir.'

At the police station he was charged. 'You realise I'll lose my job now?' he said.

'Shouldn't you have thought of that before you started drinking?'

'Oh but I did, officer, I did! Got myself a job in Pringle's Model Shop this very morning.' He began laughing and he was still laughing when a kindly neighbour came to collect him.

The Allotment Society
A novel extract
Eric McFarlane

Chapter 1

'Good morning, professor. What a beautiful day.' Daniel knew that his voice sounded bright and confident, because that was how he felt. The sun shone from a cloudless sky, at least it did in the university square outside the professor's office, he had an offer of a new job and, after two months of togetherness, Lorraine still poured milk on his morning cereal. Yes, life was definitely worth living.

Professor Quentin Farquharson, Daniel's boss, on the other hand, looked unnaturally down. He slumped in his office chair. The lines that had always creased his forehead, below the fuzz of wispy white hair, seemed criss-crossed by yet more and deeper lines. His desk was cluttered with papers and used coffee cups, indeed some of the papers appeared to have been used to mop up the contents of the cups. He gave no response to the cheery greeting.

'Professor?' Daniel fingered the resignation letter in his pocket. How to proceed? He was used to Farquharson's day to day mood swings which usually related to whether he had struck lucky the previous night. At an indeterminate seventy plus he appeared to have no difficulty in finding an inexhaustible supply of lovers to service his palaeolithic plonker. The lovers' gender or indeed species assignment seemed to concern him little.

'Professor, I came to give you...'

'Daniel, the very man.' The professor jerked into life as if someone had tugged a string. 'It's you I need.'

Daniel took a step back from the desk. 'No, really I couldn't, thanks all the same. You see I've brought my let...'

'I'm in trouble, my fair friend. I need a saviour. You are my saviour, Daniel, my rock. I knew I was right to keep you on.'

'Ah. Now wait. I don't think that's quite...'

'I refer to our understanding, Daniel, our little arrangement. I had hoped to have no further need of your expert services but, well, you have turned out to be a worthwhile insurance policy.'

'I don't... understand.'

But he had a ghastly feeling that he did in fact understand Farquharson's wittering. Well if the old fool was going to try any funny business it wasn't going to work.

'It's been a few months now since you took on the position of chief technician after the sudden resignation of dear Mr Peabrose. Oh and do sit down my boy.'

Daniel perched on the hard backed chair in front of the professor's desk and took a deep breath. 'It's been more than a year actually, professor, and I've decided on a change.' He reached into his pocket. 'Look, I have a let...'

'A year? Well, well, time flies does it not. A year, eh? And you have enjoyed your time in post?'

'Enjoyed? Well yes. I'm happy enough, it's just...'

'Happiness is a strange phenomenon. Ephemeral one might say. I too was happy, until very recently that is, until the tides of darkness washed up on my shore.'

'Tides?'

'Of darkness, yes. A poetic phrase. Too poetic for what has befallen me.'

Daniel felt his face redden. His teeth clench. He had to take control here. 'Professor. I'm sorry about your problems but I've decided to go. To leave. Another job. I have a let...'

'Leave.' The professor looked as if he had been hit by a very large object travelling very fast, possibly a meteorite of the type that had done for the dinos. 'No, no, quite impossible. Not at this moment. Oh my goodness no.'

Daniel fumbled in his pocket. 'Professor I'm sorry but my mind is made up. I've been offered a job. I'd like to give you my let...'

'Stop,' the professor boomed, raising his hand. Daniel stopped. 'We need to discuss a number of things. Things pertaining to your employment.' He rose and made his way slowly around his desk until he was behind Daniel's chair.

Daniel flinched as a cadaverous hand rested on his shoulder.

'My boy, I'm sure you will agree that I myself was instrumental in obtaining your current position for you.'

He nodded as skinny fingers worked their way round his neck.

'That without my recommendation you would in fact not have been employed again at this university.'

He cringed as skeleton digits began to massage his shoulder: those same fingers that were rumoured to have wormed their way into many an unsavoury place.

'You will remember that as part of that we came to a little agreement.'

'Well...'

'An unofficial agreement. No signatures, witnesses or anything of that sort. Just two gentlemen agreeing. Agreeing that one gentleman would help the other gentleman should that second gentleman ever have need of his services.'

'Yes, professor, I remember. But that's why I came here to tell you I have another job offer and to give you my let...'

'So my boy. I have need of your services, urgently.' The fingers squeezed firmly and then let go. He returned to his place behind his desk. 'A simple little job that is all and then you may retire to pasture's new.'

Daniel rubbed his forehead hard. The old loony wasn't going to get away with this. But before he could come up with a reply the professor continued.

'Of course should you have any difficulty with this proposition we might have to consider where we stand viz a viz certain events. I refer of course to the sad, sad death of my dear wife, Jemima.'

Daniel wanted to scream. Instead he farted, involuntarily and rather loudly. The professor looked round as if confused as to where the sound had come from.

'Professor, that's all in the past.'

To Daniel it was in the past. Far from being 'dear Jemima' the professor had very much wanted his wife dead. Unfortunately her completely accidental fall from a great height had been linked by the professor to Daniel. This had resulted in undying thanks, a bundle of used banknotes and his current situation.

'Professor, I'd love to help, but...'

'Excellent Daniel, welcome aboard.'

'No, no I meant...'

'And of course we shall say no more of the little matter of the evidence inadvertently withheld from the police all those months ago.'

'What?'

'Yes, the little matter of the photographs linking you and my dear wife Jemima, the photographs of your assignation.'

'Photographs?'

'But of course those must be destroyed. It wouldn't do for them to fall into the wrong hands would it now? Oh dear no.'

Daniel closed his eyes, breathed deeply and tried to slow his thumping heart.

'And of course they will be destroyed when you fly the nest, eventually. As soon as I have the time. Meanwhile there is this little matter. Can you help me?'

Daniel sat back in the chair. He'd been well and truly whacked. He heard a distant voice say, 'You'd better tell me about it.'

Homecoming
Jenifer Harley

A hard working man all his days
He always made a living
High above us he plied his trade
Some say without forgiving

His face reflected wind and sun
A countenance fair ruddy
Hands hacked and scraped with tile in hand
And more than often bloody

His family at home would wait
His homecoming every day
they hear it faint then louder shrill
To say He's on his way

A fine sound from a handsome man
As rugged as a thistle
I've done my shift put on my tea
said Robert's cheery whistle

Written by Jenifer Harley 2006 (Robert passed away 12 May 2006)

Mothers' day off
Anne E. Edwards

The little girl pulls exaggerated faces while her hair is brushed mercilessly, dragging through the tugs.

"Keep your socks clean, don't let your feet in the gutter, pinafore stays on till after the dinner," says mum.

"Owa owa" yelps the girl

"Nora don't fight me, it's got to be done. I'm putting a hair band on, you don't dare take it off'." Mum waits.

"Nora what do you say?" She gives the curls a particularly vicious bashing.

"Ok ok. The girl tries to wriggle out of the chair and is pushed back.

"Don't you ok, me...and keep your cardigan on, it's not to be lost. I'm not having it brought back by some Treeny Webster next week with threads pulled and it all stretched out of shape by her big girls. What do you say Nora?"

"Yes Mum, no Mum," then adds "three bags full Mum."

Her mother slaps her ear but not too hard. Nora takes this as a cue to go and grabs an empty tobacco tin from the top of the stove, puts it deep in her pocket and runs out the door into the street. She looks for the right sized stone to weight the tin. With a broken piece of lime wash she chalks numbered squares on the pavement. Two girls much the same age but not so smartly dressed watch, waiting for the invite to join in. They lean over the squares so that Nora has to dodge around them.

"What you all dressed up for Nora, going to a party?" says one.

Nora pauses. She starts to kick the can and hops behind it. She's not sure of her information and needs to get it right in her head first.

"I heard your granny is coming and you is all having a party," says the second.

"She your Lilliput granny, coming on a boat?" says the first.

"Li-thoo-ain-e-ur-a" says Nora, careful to say it the way her mum had taught her.

An impressive black car comes along the road, brazen heads poke out of doors and passages, over garden fences. The car stops outside Nora's house, the children give it Oohs and Aahs, standing round daring each other to touch it.

The driver steps out. He looks neither left nor right but goes straight to the front door, his cap still on his head. He speaks to Nora's mother at the door in quiet tones. Agnes too, starts quiet then builds up a head of steam. Everyone can hear what she says.

"The pub, the pub...she wants a wodka, she says wants a wodka. We're Temperance, she knows we're Temperance."

There are more indistinct murmurs from the driver, placating, pleading.

"It is not medicinal... I don't care how far she's travelled, she might have come from the moon!"

Then contradicting what she's just said by her actions she plonks a hat on her head and grabs her handbag, pushing the driver in front of her as she heads for the car acknowledging no one.

The first glimpse Nora has of Granny Olessa is from standing on the pub window ledge, peering in through cupped hands to minimise the reflection. Her mum and aunt hover, shielding their mother from public view as she drinks her vodka.

The next month in Dharamsala (October 2014)
Excerpt from Elizabeth Montgomery's travel blog:
Elizabeth Montgomery

It's not all sunshine and plane sailing being a traveller. Sometimes you're lucky and meet some amazing, genuine people, other times you meet some two faced ones and worse still some right tools! The eccentric ones are fun and the odd balls spice it up but I like people that you can laugh and be yourself with.

After Christina and Louise (some genuine and cool girls) I met some two faced people and found it hard to relax with them. You know the type- elitist, condescending and only in it for the chance to prove they're better than others. So one day when I was passing through Bhagsu on a path through nature (read no cars), I'd sat down on a rock to get some sun and heard some light hearted chatting at Big Mamma's Cafe. I decided to be brave and go and ask to join them.

There started my circle of Dharamsala buddies, with Jeanie from Idaho and Katherine from French Canada. Jeanie is a sweet lass on a two year adventure travelling the world, who loves food and puppies, so there's three things in common! Katherine was wearing a really funky turquoise ring made out of a recycled fork and in my book, recycled art wearers equals good people and she is also a fellow blogger which is always inspiring to meet people doing what you want to do! Katherine introduced us to Michael from Boston who she'd worked with in some crazy bus driving capacity and tree planting shenanigans. He is all about Eco living and sustainability and is a fellow wwoofer (willing workers on organic farms)! And Michael in turn brought along Ian (pronounced eyun) from the Philippines who spent most of his spare time Skyping his fiancé, videoing amazing scenery and doing handstands at breathtaking places. In between hanging out with this

78

bunch and making silver jewellery I really loved attending a 9.30am drop in meditation class at a Buddhist place called Tushita.

It was usually two sets of 24 minutes meditation where you can stretch in the middle and ask questions at the end. I had two teachers in my time there, one quite jolly guy who often touched on depressing topics but always managed to rein it in at the end so I left feeling light hearted and at peace. He'd say 'everyone wants to be happy and not wants to suffer' excessively. And the second a rather good looking guy who did a four day sequential meditation session that was really powerful teaching compassion, equanimity, and love and kindness which culminated with the three topics on the fourth day, breathing in smoke and dispelling it then breathing out light and love.

Tushita was at the top of a hill surrounded by pine trees and monkeys. One morning I was hungry so nonchalantly bought a banana for breakfast, as you do in these parts, totally forgetting about the cheeky monkeys. Too late; one spotted me. I quickly munched the banana and chucked the skin down the hill which managed to divert him and left me to finish my breakfast. Phew! I love monkeys but I've seen them stealing food from people and it's not polite.

After meditations I had plenty of time to walk around in nature, make jewellery and look around all the magical streets in McLeod Ganj. But we'd usually end up in Welcome Cafe in upper Bhagsu. My first night I walked in with Jeanie and Gopish, our new friend, originally from Dubai but living in Mumbai who is a motorcycle fanatic, hotel management student, sweet toothed, sweet guy. It was like stepping into another time and place, UV and coloured spot lights dotted the room.

A mural of a hand holding an eye and two mushrooms adorned the counter, another one of a man smoking a chillum (pipe) covered the speaker, and of course the obligatory mural of Bob Marley.

We were welcomed to sit at the front table or more like squeezed into among all the people. There was a three piece band consisting drums, bass and a guitar/singer singing about Arabian nights and living in the desert and finding a good husband. I found this strange being in India, considering I'd just spent four years in love with Dahab a desert paradise on the Red Sea in Egypt. It's funny what speaks to you and when.

I later learned that the singer, Kern from Delhi, was just singing off the top of his head. We later became really good friends as he is spiritual and opened me up to a few truths and reacquainted me with EFT (Emotional Freedom Technique or Tapping). He wears his hair in dreads and has a laid back vibe about him.

Bhagsu is up in the Himalayan Mountains and the evenings were starting to get fresh. Ginger lemon honey was the drink to drink, with choruses from Chandan the funky, hippy, waiter singing out all night to the kitchen and dancing round the room taking orders. When one guys order came out and I'd seen him leave, the whole room was chanting 'ginger lemon honey' culminating in Kern also incorporating it into his jam (song). I never had a tastier one anywhere.

We also went to Om Cafe one evening for a 'dance your pants off' party, and that's what everyone did, lots of drumming, singing and dancing.

As there is no meditation on at Tushita on a Sunday, the five of us decided to hike up Triund the looming mountain in the background surrounded by snow capped peaks. We had plans to leave early but by the time we'd all had breakfast it was 9.30am. The way was quite gruelling with plenty steep bits and paths made of boulders. We stopped to take in the view and chat or drink chai. The view over the whole of Dharamsala is spectacular. You can see each village, Bhagsu on the left, Dharamkot the right, McLeod

Ganj around the hill in the middle and Dharamsala town off in the background.

There are birds of prey circling around, small pink flowers like liquorice all sorts (sweets/candy), goats and a few monkeys! The most picturesque view came around a corner when you can see the snow capped tip in full sun and now we know it's not far to go.

The last part is the hardest as the snow capped peak disappears and we have to zig zag through forest, which is a welcome shade and cool breeze, and rocky paths. Ian, who is a free runner, was rock climbing shortcuts. I tried a few until my camera fell from my pocket. The last half hour was the worst, heavy breathing, no more smiling or chatting and people coming down kept saying, 'You're almost there, not long to go, 15-10 minutes'. We then popped out on top of a grassy area with cows, tourists, and blue tarpaulin tents selling drinks, snacks and hot food.

If the weather turns bad or you leave too late in the day there are tents and sleeping bags for rent. There's a temple a little further up at the snow line but there's not enough time and I'm too knackered to go, maybe next time! I lie in the grass and watch the birds circling above in the gorgeous blue sky. Clouds move in and we eat some rice and Dahl (lentils). A cow moves from bag to bag searching for food. A few dogs followed people up, whoever they felt good with. It's taken us three and a half hours to reach the top and Ian still has the energy to do some handstands at the view point with the shear drop. Brave!

On the descent we find some baby goats who have been trapped under a rock, literally closed in under an overhang. The cafe guy keeps having to tell people it's ok and to leave them. The shepherd put them there to protect them from falling or being eaten: like a crèche.

Good thing about hiking or any physical exercise is that you can treat yourself after. In Bhagsu there is a small restaurant called

Dodo Falafel where alongside the best falafel in town you can also get Snickers chapati, or Mars, Milkyway, Bounty, any chocolate bar really. It's rolled up in a chapati deep fried and then covered in Nutella. Delicious! One afternoon Jeanie and I met Kern and Gopish in Dodo Falafel. After filling our tummies with, you guessed it, falafel and Snickers chapati, we strolled through Bhagsu and up to the top of the waterfall. It was a misty day and rain threatened but never really came. You could see our breath as we were literally inside the cloud. At the very top we sought shelter in a restaurant and drank the world's smallest ginger lemon honey and played Carrum.

It's a bit like pool but you use your finger to flick the big chip to pot the smaller chips. There are 12 white chips worth 10 points, 3 black chips worth 20 points and 1 red one worth 50 points. You can play two ways: wait till the end to pot the red or if you pot it you have to pot a white after. If you accidentally pot the big chip you have to put one of your winning chips back on the board and if you pot one you get another go. At one point I potted a few really fast in a row but in the end Kern won. And that's today's lesson, if you want to win in life you have to really believe you've already won.

The Snails Move Out
Ian Macartney

Rain made the spiral houses
part away from each other
on gelatinous railways.
A town disbanded.

They backpacked
across the pavement with
staircases on their backs.

Slugging through pools of their own body,
their Golden Ratios got crushed by feet
from down south.
Living-rooms flooded in downpour,
tear-drop Recessions.
Fibonacci caved in.

The mangled fluid
turned clay-red.
The others had to go,
before the eels they built their houses on
swam away in the flying water.

Truth
Inspired by Light the Way by Leslie Moroney
(http://spontaneity.org/issue01/still-life/)
Stephen Shirres

Eilidh read over the letter for the final time before she folded it in two and placed it inside the envelope that lay on her bed covers. The dry glue felt rough on her drier tongue. She'd never liked the taste of envelopes. Her mum had once hit for spitting out the taste when she was young.

She picked up the foundation pen from her bedside table and with shaking hands wrote two names on the brown surface: Menzies and Millicent. Out of habit she blew the ink dry and kissed Menzies' name. Dots of pink lipstick now surrounded her son's name. The effect made her give a chuckle that turned into a cough. A mouthful of water helped to fend off the attack.

Her walls were covered in photos of happy memories and shapes of yellow light, refractions created by the water glass and her bedside light. Each photo was filled with happy memories: ice creams at the beach, holidays and trips. All contained the same smile from her boy. She noticed for the first time that she'd put them in age order. From left to right he grew older.

Her hand reached for the third object that lived on her bedside, a small bell that had followed her from house to house since her fifth birthday. Until recently it had been a welcome companion. Now it summed up her frailties. She rung it twice. The gentle ring echoed through the small house before being drowned out by the crash of a pair of boots on the wooden floor downstairs. Menzies had his feet up on the sofa again. Eilidh knew she should tell him off but she didn't have the energy or the desire to do so. The boots crashed up the stairs. Eilidh half expected a young boy to open the door to her bedroom. Instead it revealed a man in his twenties, Menzies, sporting an unshaven face with unkempt hair. She'd made the right choice all those years ago. For the final time Eilidh smiled.

The mist seeped into Menzies' clothing. Water dripped from his uncut hair and glasses. Not for the first time he wished he used the contact lenses that sat unopened at home. He gave a sniff of laughter. The small house didn't feel like home any more. The last of her warmth was in her letter which he carried in his duffel coat pocket. Eilidh's handwriting was already bad enough without water damage making the ink run and splodge.

Above him lamps hung from the black trees. The light they admitted fuzzed into the mist. They led him to a thick black stripe that ran across the horizon. The only gap bridged by a metal arch. Dark vines weaved between rusted letters.

Inside the wall a new shape dominated the landscape, a mansion whose only distinctive feature was its size. From almost the middle of the building, two dim circles glowed, like a pair of sad eyes. Menzies hoped the outside of the mansion wasn't a metaphor for those inside. The mansion's door completed the face. The slab of wood was the same shade as the stone work that surrounded it. The bronze knocker at least gave it some character. Menzies reached for the heavy metal hoop. He hesitated and decided to knock. His fist fell hard, too hard, on the weathered wood. The sound echoed inside. He added a couple of short knocks to try and make his first attempt sound more natural. He was sure he failed.

The door slid open silently to reveal an old man in a dark suit. A hint of dust on his shoulders. Everything about him could be described as old, tall and thin, even the words that escaped his lips. "Hello?"

"Hi." Menzies replied.

The old man looked down at him. His nose filled his face. Menzies wanted to take a step back but he knew if he did he'd never stop. He counted to ten as his mum had told him to do.

"I have a message for M...for Millicent."

"Well..." The old man seemed to pause for longer than normal. "...this way."

Inside the house was lit by the same lamps as outside. This time they hung on the walls rather than above. Their light created pools of yellow where the oak panelled walls met the black red carpet. Dark paintings of hunts interrupted the oak panelling, a scared fox the only splash of bright colour. Only the first door they passed was open. Inside was a high back chair and an old fashioned music system. From the speakers Vivaldi's Winter Concerto escaped and creeped after the pair as they turned into new corridors. Menzies quickly felt lost, each corridor looked the same. The final one they turned into had only one door. The old man stopped in front of it and knocked twice. Both were polite as he wished to gain a person's attention but not annoy them. Inside, the excited whispers of two female voices stopped as if turned off by a switch to be replaced by a single groan which lasted for only a moment.

"Come," a female voice beckoned. The old man pushed the door open, ushered Menzies to go in before he turned and walked away. Menzies took a deep breath and stepped inside.

The room felt as large as the house itself. In the centre was a giant four poster bed, purple curtains tied to each post. The far wall was taken up by a fire place that stretched from one side of the room to the other. Above it was an equally big TV. The screen was filled with the image of a blonde haired young woman's head and bare shoulders. Menzies wondered if this was the case for the rest of her body. Her lips were formed into the shape of a frozen kiss being blown at the viewer. The same face appeared from the bed, much less happy. Her blonde hair swept over her shoulders. She looked at Menzies, her face filled with challenge. It soften when a hand appeared from behind her and was placed on her shoulder. The red nails were stark against the woman's pale skin. The rest of the woman appeared from behind the younger one. She was twice as old but as beautiful. A silk gown decorated, rather than covered her body. Millicent, Menzies thought as he averted his eyes. .

"Yes?" Millicent asked, the same voice that had told him to enter.

"I have a message for you." Menzies was surprised his voice was so confident. "From Eilidh."

Millicent turned to the blonde. "Go," she instructed.

"But..."

"Now." She emphasised the syllable.

The blonde lifted herself off the bed and walked towards Menzies, answering his earlier thought in the process. When she reached him, she grabbed his face and pulled it towards her lips, kissing him hard. The surprise was replaced with the pleasure of her soft lips. She broke the kiss and shouted at Millicant, "gone."

The door echoed as it slammed into its frame.

"She'll be back." Millicent stepped off the bed. "What was your message?"

Menzies had practised his response to this question over and over since he had first read the letter, yet the words turned into misshapen lumps in his mouth.

"Well?" So much contempt in a small word.

He swallowed before saying, "Eilidh died this morning."

Millicent's face didn't react, instead she picked up a cigarette from the mantelpiece behind her and lit it on the fire. After a single drag she said, "I'm sorry to hear that. I'd heard she was ill."

"Very ill."

"Clearly."

Menzies clinched his fists in anger. His nails dug into his palm as he fought to keep his emotion there.

"She," his voice cracked, "...left this." Menzies pulled the letter from his jacket pocket and threw it on the floor in front of her where it landed with a satisfying thump. Small brown water stains marked the edges. One side had been ripped open and now looked like a mountain range covered in a snow of torn paper. "For you...for us."

"What does it say?" Millicent blew the toxins of her cigarette into the air between them.

"The truth." Menzies cursed himself for saying something so corny. The word undermined the importance of the situation, of what he was about to say. "That you are my mother."

The cigarette dropped from Millicent's fingers. It rested on the floor, the ash mixing with the carpet. Without looking, and with perfect precision, she flicked it into the fire behind with her foot. She pulled her gown around her body covering up the skin she had on show. She stepped forward and took the letter from Menzies's outstretched hand. "Now you know. Eilidh was always..." Millicent stopped as if her next words needed careful consideration to protect herself rather than him, "...More caring, the better mother."

"I know." Anger slipped into his words. "I'm only doing what Eilidh...mum asked." The final word washed across the room to reveal the situation in its true form. The only reason why Menzies was here was gone. Millicent didn't seem to want to provide another.

The door echoed for the second time that night. This time silence followed. Millicent sat down on the edge of the bed, her back to the door, the fire in front of her. She smiled at her schoolfriend's handwriting, slanted lines and non-existent loops decorated the

88

page. The words were equally distinctive, all kindness where none was due. For Menzies' benefit Millicent hoped. When she had finished reading, she lifted the letter to her lips and kissed Eilidh's signature.

"Goodbye old friend." She folded the letter back into the envelope and placed it into the fire where the flames turned her old life into ash.

Winter Traveler

Chris Gorman

It was late autumn, although both the climate and the landscape said winter had come early to this very northerly latitude. The deciduous trees were already bare. The ground was hard but the short grass was still free of snow. The sun was shining but it was low in the sky and the air was very cold.

He contemplated the journey ahead. He had made this journey before: many times in fact, and always at this time of year. It may take twenty two sunsets until he reached his destination. As he set off he felt light-hearted and not too concerned about weather conditions. He could see that the evergreen trees were plenty and that they would provide some shelter from worse conditions, such as the biting wind, that was sure to cross the path of his odyssey. After an hour or so he began to think that his state of fitness was not quite what it should be. He had spent many days just lazing around and some of the rich pickings that he had enjoyed had not been accompanied by enough exercise. Not that he had overeaten. Maybe the extra fat he carried could serve him well in the days to come as the journey became more arduous.

By the end of that first day he felt tired and a little concerned that he had not gone as far as he might have hoped. He lay near the shelter of a giant fir and was soon asleep. The next day he awoke early and, after some breakfast, set off again. He felt quite invigorated and thought that, if anything, it was a little warmer that day. Over days two, three and four his progress was good and he felt good in himself. His fitness was returning to what was required for the task he was undertaking. Although, as he had previously noted, the deciduous trees were stripped of their finery, holly bushes abounded and each bore a mass of shiny red berries.

90

The little creatures will benefit from these ripe little treasures, he thought. *Isn't nature wonderful in its balance?*

Into the fifth day and he began to notice how much shorter the daylight hours had become and that the temperature was steadily dropping. However it was still dry, not too much wind and progress was good. He was glad of his heavy warm coat. Day six and it began to rain. The wind picked up and blew straight into his face. Wind on its own would be bad enough but, with this rain, visibility was poor. On the seventh day there was no rain and the wind had dropped; so had the temperature. Late in the day it began to snow light feathery flakes. He knew that the landscape would soon turn completely white but this was better than that driving rain. Days eight, nine, ten and eleven, the snow turned to blizzard and the wind became ferocious. This really slowed him down and indeed most of the eleventh day he spent sheltering beneath a partially fallen evergreen he found in a little wooded area. This also provided him some well earned rest since the two previous days had involved some heavy going through very open country. He made sure he ate well that day because, no matter the conditions, he would have to set off again in the morning.

Eleven sunsets since I started out, he thought to himself that night as he lay down to sleep. *I've taken up half the time and I sense that I've covered less than half the distance. I'll have to push myself tomorrow and in the days to come.*

Next morning the wind was gone, the sun was shining and it was with renewed hope that he set off. It didn't feel so cold and there was little wind to impede his progress. However, the snow now lay thick and deep and walking through it proved to be exhausting. After a while he realised that the other factor which was slowing him down was that he was walking up a gradual incline. Ahead he could see white, white, white with some clear blue sky above.

Occasionally some large birds, eagles or the like would drift across the skyline. At last he came to the top of the ridge and was able to look down a long slope to a familiar landscape. At the bottom was a forest that he recognised. He decided to risk a little adventure and he threw himself into a slide down the hill. To one less experienced the speed that he reached would have been frightening but he felt confident and thought of the time that this would make up for his slow climb. As he approached the trees he saw that the snow on the ground was thinner and he followed a little stream that flowed in a slightly twisted path through the forest.

It was like this through day thirteen to nineteen and he began to feel sure that he would make it in the time he had allowed. Food was running low but there was a plentiful supply of water from the little stream. It was certainly much better than the snow he had been eating before and on one occasion when he stopped to drink he thought back to summer. The water's extreme coolness would have been welcomed for that quality back in those warm summer and early autumn days but in this climate it made his teeth chatter.

Still, at least it's wet and thirst quenching, he thought and almost lay down in the snow to rest as visions of those days of long sunshine floated through his mind.

But he quickly pulled himself up. It would be dangerous to fall asleep here. On he trudged and on day twenty he started to emerge from the trees and back into the open. The wind had picked up again and he really felt in now. The woods had provided shelter from the worst of the wind but now it picked up drifting snow and blew it into his eyes, ears and mouth. He was starting to feel exhausted and extremely hungry. However, he had his warm coat and he knew he was on schedule and that good days lay ahead. These thoughts kept him going through the twenty first and twenty second days.

Towards the end of that day, as the sun was going down, he spotted some ghostly white trees in the distance. As he got closer, a thin wisp of grey smoke could be seen above the tree line, climbing into the darkening sky. Life! Nearer still and he saw a small clearing in the trees. Gradually the shape of a little wooden house emerged. He began to hear happy noises and, as he rounded a bend into the clearing, bright lights streamed from the windows. He was almost there and he thought about the comfortable warm bed he would have that night; the first in twenty two days. Just at that point a figure emerged from the little house. He was still a good ways off and he could not quite determine the identity of the man, but drawing closer he recognised the main features. It was a little old man with a round belly and a long white beard. When close enough to see the face, he saw the old man wipe his eyes and just at that point his face lit up.

The old saint stretched his arms wide and exclaimed, "Prancer, my dear old friend, I was beginning to worry. But here you are and, as usual, the first to arrive."

He encircled the reindeer's neck with his arms and Prancer nuzzled his face into the old man's thick warm coat. "Come into the warm barn my friend. We have a feast prepared for you. I expect the others will be arriving soon. It's now the twenty first of December, so you will have a good two days' rest before our busiest day of the year."

Later, the old man again embraced his four legged friend and whispered affectionately in his ear, "You've lost a lot of weight on your long journey, you brave old boy, but we'll soon fatten you up and have you fighting fit."

Prancer was asleep within seconds of his head touching the warm straw that night and he dreamed of the fun days ahead.

Contributing Writers

Sue Davies
Sue has lived her 40 yrs of married life in West Lothian and before she retired she was a nurse in a care home. The attempt to use words to picture and treasure the beauty of living things, people and places the motivation for writing.

Anne E. Edwards
Anne E. Edwards can't remember a time when she wasn't writing something, filling little notebooks with stories. She has the luxury of free time now and enjoys being a member of West Lothian Writers and going on poetry retreats. Anne is presently secretary of West Lothian Writers

Norman Geddes
Norman is a recently retired driving examiner who has lived in West Lothian for the past 43 years. He is married with two daughters and a recently acquired granddaughter. Writing fiction is his principal hobby.

Chris Gorman
After a working life that often included writing formal (i.e. boring) papers, Chris wanted to try his hand at something for fun. His main artistic pursuits are in painting and photography but loves many other genres including literature. drama and music. He has had a go at short story writing, the odd poem and one or two aborted attempts at a longer novel.

Elizabeth Hands
Elizabeth Hands lives in Armadale

Jenifer Harley

Originally from East Lothian but has made Livingston home since 1977. Married to Dave, she has two sons, both married, and one grandson whom she adores. Writing is her passion and she loves being part of West Lothian Writers but rarely enters competitions or submits her work. Maybe next year she will remedy this."

Ian Macartney

Ian Macartney is a 16-year old Scottish writer. He has been a Prizewinner in the Pushkin Prizes 2012, RSPB's Wildverse 2012 and Foyle Young Poets 2015 (he was Commended Position in Foyle Young Poets 2014). He also also written the scripts for two short films, Decko and Anhedonia, both of which are available on YouTube. He resides in Linlithgow

Eric McFarlane

Eric McFarlane has written for as long as he can remember. Genre fiction whether novel or short story length is his first love and he has written humour, SF, crime and horror. He has completed several novels and many short stories some of which have been published online and in print.

His comic crime novel 'A Clear Solution' has recently been published by Accent Press.

www.ericmcfarlane.co.uk

www.facebook.com/EricMcFarlaneAuthor

Susi Moffat

Susan Moffat has been a member of West Lothian Writers for six years, initially writing fantasy novels. However, with university, a job, a wedding, and a new baby also filling those years, she has recently been focussing on writing comic and fantasy short stories.

Elizabeth Montgomery

An adventurer, someone who seeks. A wanderer, a dreamer, a make believer. One who writes, paints, creates, sings, dances and twirls her hair. To connect find her at betsybluetoes.wordpress.com although some would say she's elusive.

Stephen Shirres

Stephen is a writer of short stories and stories that are shorter of almost any genre or style. It all depends what takes his fancy at the time. When he isn't writing he is chairing West Lothian Writers

W. T. Sutherland

W. T. Sutherland, known as Bill at West Lothian Writers, is a retired jeweller in his retirement started to write as a hobby. His first book "Journey to Altnagar" he wrote based on his love of the highlands of Scotland and having been read by some friends he was encouraged to publish on Amazon. Although not a great seller, has sold in many countries from the USA to France.

Sally Thomson

Sally Thomson writes mainly poetry, flash fiction and children's stories when she finds a few spare moments in between working full time and bringing up her three young boys. This is also one of the reasons her work is short!. Her work is often inspired by nature, being out doors and her children.

Margaret Walker

Margaret has always loved books and has been writing stories from an early age. She has written a collection of "cat" stories based on the antics of various pets belonging to her and to friends and neighbours. She has only recently joined West Lothian Writers but it has helped her very much – it is hard to be your own critic.

About West Lothian Writers

West Lothian Writers (WLW) was formed in 2006 when the West Lothian College Writers group left its based at West Lothian College and set out on their own. Since then the group has gone from strength to strength. We presently have a large and engaged membership that has allowed us to create projects such as the book you are presently reading.

WLW meets every second Tuesday to offer advice and support to local amateur writers who make up our memberships. Members are encouraged to bring along pieces of writing, up to 1500 words, which they read out and then receive feedback on the piece. A wide range of work is heard every meeting including short stories, poetry, novel extracts and script excerpts.

We also regularly invite published writers to present workshops and provide their own professional feedback on our work. Janis Mackay and David Bishop are just a few of the people who have come along to one of our meetings to delivery workshops on writing.

To find out more about West Lothian Writers please check out our website at http://www.westlothianwriters.org.uk.

The Successes of West Lothian Writers
Stephen Shirres

One of the reasons why we decided to publish these anthologies is to promote the work of our members. Many of whom have never been published before.

Those who have been published have been so in a large range of magazines and websites across the planet. Eric has had his comic Seline stories published in Smashwords and ABC Tales while some of his more serious work has appeared in Devilfish Review and Ironstone. Eric isn't the only member of WLW to grace the pages of Ironstone as Anne, Jenifer and Norman have also had work published by them. Stephen has been published in a similar range of magazines including Untitled, Anti-Zine Far Off Places and Spontaneity, where his story Truth was published.

Our members have also had their novels published. Bill has self published a couple of his novels on Amazon, Aftermath and Journey to Altnager which have been purchased in France and the USA. This year has also seen Eric have his first novel, A Clear Solution, published by Accent Press. It is available now from www.ericmcfarlane.co.uk.

West Lothian Writers also contains its fair share of competition winners. Jenifer won My Kind of Town where you had to write a poem about a town in Scotland. Her winning entry was printed onto a set of special pint glass. You can find her poem on our website www.westlothianwriters.org.uk. Towards the end of 2014 Stephen won the 99 Fiction Flash 500 competition with his story Absorbing Art. Our most recent competition winner was Ian Macartney who won one of the 15 prizes in the Foyle Young Poets 2015 competition with his poem The Snails Move Out which has been included in this collection. There were over 6000 entries this year.

Finally, we can't talk about the success of West Lothian Writers without touching upon What To Do About Mum? In 2014 Anne Edwards self funded her own play written about her experiences of her Mum's Alzheimers. The play was performed on 30th of March to a sold out crowd at the Bathgate Regal. There has been talk of other performances of What To Do About Mum? but availability issues has stopped these from happening so far.

West Lothian Writers Workshops
Susan Moffat

West Lothian Writers hosts regular workshops led by guest authors. Recently, I had the privilege of attending two of these workshops; one on World Building, and one on performing our written work aloud.

In April, we were lucky enough to have David Bishop (who has written novels as well as for TV and radio) run a tutorial on World Building. Although this may sound like a very sci-fi focussed workshop, it was actually suitable for writers of almost any genre.

David described 'world building' as creating a credible backdrop for your fiction. In other words, highlighting the differences between your fictional world and the real world, and working out how these differences affect the people and the look of your world. For example, if you make everyone in your world is pathologically shy, how does that impact on your world and the people in it; what happens when they meet? How do they get the food and services they require? Also, are there still cinemas, restaurants, schools etc?

To make a world realistic, David reports that it is essential to have rules and restraints. For example, in a world where there is magic there has to be limits, otherwise there would be no drama or conflict around which to base the story as everyone could solve all their problems instantly.

In order to understand this need for rules and restraints, we participated in a group exercise where we had to describe the consequences of a world where everyone has the same superpower. My group discussed a world where all the inhabitants are able to control others with their minds. Very quickly we realised the importance of placing limitations on this ability because without restraints our world would descend into chaos and destroy itself. It was also really interesting thinking about how the addition of one extra ability would drastically alter the world. For example, would good or evil people dominate? How would people protect themselves from the influence of others?

Another way to add realism to your writing is to use all five senses (or as many as possible) when describing your world. The second exercise completed during the workshop focussed on thinking about the five senses and what they would detect about our superpower world. This was quite a challenging exercise because I mainly focus on sight, sound and smell when writing. It was difficult to imagine how the world would feel and smell when there were so many unanswered questions about exactly how our world would function. This exercise really made me think about how much thought I have to put into my writing to make it realistic.

During the workshop David also discussed the importance of using a light touch when world building by providing only essential information and drip-feeding the reader; choosing what to reveal and when. In other words, don't simply explain all about your world in a paragraph at the start, let the reader find out some things about the world through the language and slang used, the architecture of the world, and the characters' actions and behaviour. Due to this a lot of world building is character-led, with their use of language, their thoughts and actions.

The second workshop I attended was in June when Polly Phillps held a Performance Workshop for a small group of members. This workshop aimed to increase our confidence and skills when performing our writing aloud. In preparation for the class, we all brought a short piece of our own writing to read aloud in front of the rest of the group.

At the start of the workshop we were all asked to write down three words that we would use to describe ourselves. These were then shared with the rest of the group who commented on whether this was also their perception of that individual. This was a very interesting exercise; I described myself as shy, nervous and not confident, however, others in the group were surprised by this as this did not match their perception of me. They did not class me as any of those three things, perhaps showing that I manage to project a different image when reading my work aloud.

We then took turns at reading our work aloud and commenting on others strengths and weaknesses. Polly then made suggestions to improve our performance; altering the speed of our speech, suggesting gestures, adjusting our stance etc. After the initial reading, we practiced altering our voices by making our voice come from different parts of our vocal system. I found this aspect particularly challenging as I have not studied music or singing before and struggled to understand how to control different muscles as I have not used them intentionally before.

After learning how to alter our voices, we had to read our piece again using different vocal registers and gestures. I felt that this exercise was very challenging and that it forced people out of their comfort zone. However, I could certainly see the benefits of learning to use gestures and different vocal registers when performing.

This workshop was simply a taster session; it would take much time and practise to learn the skills touched on. However, it was highly enjoyable and I felt that I learned a lot from attending. I would certainly attend this workshop again if it was repeated in the future.

Lightning Source UK Ltd.
Milton Keynes UK
UKHW021310231220
375707UK00009B/328